A TALENT
FOR TROUBLE

MICHELA MORELLATO

authorHOUSE

AuthorHouse™
1663 Liberty Drive
Bloomington, IN 47403
www.authorhouse.com
Phone: 1 (800) 839-8640

This is a work of fiction. All of the characters, names, incidents, organizations, and dialogue
in this novel are either the products of the author's imagination or are used fictitiously.

Published by AuthorHouse 10/31/2019

ISBN: 978-1-7283-3377-9 (sc)
ISBN: 978-1-7283-3375-5 (hc)
ISBN: 978-1-7283-3376-2 (e)

Library of Congress Control Number: 2019917805

Print information available on the last page.

This book is printed on acid-free paper.

DEDICATION

This book is dedicated to my parents,
my husband and my children.

This book wouldn't have been possible
without the support of my friends:

Jason Winstanley, for his energy and creativity,
Maurizio Lullo, for encouraging me never to give up,
Michele Anoardi, for not abandoning me when times were hard

...and last but not least my best friend *Amy Braley* that in this myriad
of fortunate and unfortunate events she appeared in my life as a loyal
anchor that represents the symbol of our indissoluble friendship.

Evil is not only a disease of the afflicted but a curse on those who witness evil and let it escape.

CHAPTER 1

MY NAME IS EVA.

When I was about five, Mom found an old book of Aesop's fables in the attic. Over the next few nights, and for months afterwards, she avidly read those tales to me. I closed my eyes, as I let the sound of her comforting voice carry me to Aesop's ethereal world. In that universe, I learnt for the first time about humans and their souls. It was the perfect lesson for a curious kid like me. My favourite tale was about a farmer who saved a snake, only to be bitten to death by it. Mom highlighted the cruelty of the snake and how the farmer had his generosity betrayed, but in my heart, I couldn't feel anything but mercy for that poor animal. As a child, I came to understand the blurred contour between the victims and oppressors. This *fine line* between light and dark, fantasy and reality, cruelty and compassion, as well as beauty and ugliness, has always been an essential test in my private and public life.

Since my family lived in the hills, I had the perfect opportunity, observing the little pests; how these serpents slithered and stalked for sustenance, enjoying the sun before slinking back to their shelter. Into safety. I detested those who, out of wild brutality, would crush their poor heads under their heels. Whenever I reacted, the other kids would mock me. I felt closer to the poor reptile than those morons who claimed to be human beings. I suppose I always felt a fish out of water, twitching and thrashing on the shore for oxygen, rarely understood or accepted by the people around me. Even at that impressionable age, I knew only too well about the people and their perks in this little Venetian town I was living.

Indeed, the hills provided me with the perfect vantage point, to observe and study nature, and to let my thoughts roam freely with the clouds.

Mom was a teacher in a small school, deep in the mountains, where people barely spoke Italian. To this day they still prefer our old, regional Veneto dialect. For years, my only friends were Filippo and Giorgio, and of course, my siblings. Despite this, however, my soul would ache with indescribable solitude. I would invent friends and new adventures, like an Aesop fable. My most faithful companions at that time were a lion and a deer. There we'd be, intentionally lost in the woods around the house, which to my creative mind had become the lost kingdoms of my imagination. Inside our adventures, we'd observe the world together, watching how these dark woods would occasionally be caressed by the sunrays, sneaking through the leaves, transforming everything they touched into an enchanted paradise. There I was, standing in the middle, with the hunter on my right and the hunted on the left. Never alone. Daydreaming. Watching. Waiting.

In those days I was fragile, introverted, and loved to meddle with the unknown. In winter I slept with the window open. I would stare at the sky, trying to communicate with someone or something else beyond. I guess it must have been rough on my folks, not understanding my existential crisis. "I often encountered the ill of living", Eugenio Montale once wrote. I think it happened to me as well. Although I managed to overcome my fears, the price was high. Every day, I still feel the need to understand and judge the people around me. If there's an itch, I must scratch it, if there's a fire, I want to pass my fingers through the flame.

"The factory's done for."

Dad's words should have frozen the world around me but I didn't worry too much. Why would I? As the hormones whizzed through my body, I was lost in my emotional, highschool teen dramas. I was convinced that Dad would start up again, perhaps embarking on a new entrepreneurial activity that would have allowed us to maintain what was always a fixed standard for us: a beautiful home, a new car every year, the latest fashions and holidays at will, wherever we pleased. I hugged him hard but I didn't think he really needed it. I trusted him. He would make it right, like he always did. Like the magician he was. Dad had always worked hard. It couldn't be that difficult exploring new ventures and pastures, in such a booming economy, as it was in those days, in the north east of Italy. His skills and cunning would prove that this situation was only a minor setback. We'd roll with the punches, pick ourselves up, dust ourselves down and turn this thing around.

It was not to be. New business ideas came and went, and before we knew it, the bailiffs had no other choice than to repossess our possessions. They took everything: the furniture, the luxury cars, even the bike that Dad loved, almost as much as his own children. The house was empty, and the walls which hosted the luxuries of our former life, were now echoing the sighs of my mom. Almost overnight, the vibrant colours of family life, the annual festivities and vivacious vitality had faded into a colourless space. Where there had been humour, laughter and safety, now pervaded anxiety, subdued tears and insecurity; although you wouldn't have been able to tell that by looking at Mom and Dad. Italians have always been cloaked by a protective sheath we call the *bella figura*. Whenever you walk in any Italian city centre, you feel as if you're lost in a carnival or a fashion parade. Everywhere you go you see beautiful fashions and painted faces, smeared over grotesque smiling masks. Italians will do anything to hide away from weakness and reality. In Italy, shame and pity are considered more detestable and repugnant than envy or greed. You can have the greatest intellect and virtuous nature, but if your shoes are scuffed or out of season, you can kiss goodbye to those cherished dinner invitations. Many vices are forgivable in Italy, but once you're branded as shameful or pitiful you are finished. The light you once radiated is switched off.

Living in such a vast but empty house became not just depressing, but also expensive. My folks' optimism, to be able to turn this situation around, was just a facade. Dad's business associates also weren't taking their responsibilities seriously, leaving everyone at the mercy of the inevitable bankruptcy. If anyone could have helped, they sure as hell weren't stepping up. As for friends? Well, as we know, when things are going well, friends and good intentions swarm around us like locusts. While we toast their friendship, they are secretly feasting on our fruits and crops. When we are laughing and creating new memories with them, they are secretly gossiping or plotting against us. We believe their promises to always be around when times are rough. We believe their lies. Evidently, our friends screwed us over. I felt angry, sick and helpless. The house had become, not just a prison but a *burden*. Everything in that place that had been pulsating and effervescent became miserable and mournful. My relationship with Dad was strained. I remember his endless insistence on telling me that he did everything for the family and that we would be united and carefree again, but I couldn't see it. I had to accept, for all our sakes, that out there, beyond the mountains, existed a lousy, unjust world. No world is as cruel, I guess, than the world of business; the arena where nature plays its punishing hunger games. In this world, we have to be on guard. We must fight. We must survive.

As things got worse by the day, I lost my natural serenity and interest in simple pleasures. I can't say if it was my hormones, but I sure was a grouchy, snappy teen, furious with those who slandered my family at every turn. The world around me, that had once seemed magical and fairytale-like, had become a volatile volcano; unsympathetic, unpredictable and ready to explode. The only defense in this infernal world was to react with aggressive determination, making myself *intentionally* unpleasant. I wondered if this impulsive, hot-blooded creature was the real me, or maybe some kind of demon who wore my skin. I couldn't help but act with *fury* towards people's brutality and hypocrisy. I began to view the world, not as a safe space that liberated imagination and contentment, but as a hazardous, *toxic*, risky, no-go area, where every act and decision came with hidden dangers. To protect myself from a dangerous world, I had to become *more* dangerous.

As you can imagine, my studies were also affected. I grew short with the touchy teachers, who should have been helping me reach my potential. They were supposed to be opening my mind and enabling me to build a strong foundation; instead of doing all they could to close me down and to shut me away from education. They were numb to my problems, certainly too big for a teenager to deal with. It was a disaster. I was just as much a prisoner in school as my own home. Where was my life going?

CHAPTER 2

G RANDMOTHER USED TO SAY that you need to adjust your sails so you can take all the winds in life. She was the kind of optimistic old lady who loved making everyone comfortable. It didn't take me long to realize that she was talking about flexibility and adaptability. If we don't evolve, we die out. I had every intention of not going under, not giving an inch and taking what I needed to survive, by *any means necessary.* If people were ruthless, I had to be more ruthless. If they were merciless, I had to be more merciless. By contrast, if people are generous and loyal to me, I can be an indispensable friend for life. It works both ways. I have always been controversial: there are those who love me and those who can't stand me. No middle ground. Even today, these views of me still persist and I don't see the point of shrinking away and doing what people tell me to do. I've never had much time for prudes and snobs. These repressed bags of wind are jealous because they can't escape from the restraints of their shapewear and loveless, empty lives; living for a tomorrow that never comes.

Among those who hated me, when I was growing up, were the teachers at the School of Arts. At my school they often left the students unattended for several hours. They were supposed to sign the attendance register for the school, thus proving that for every hour there was a teacher accountable for maintaining safety and order in the classroom. No doubt, they were probably in the staffroom gossiping about the parents or having a sneaky cigarette. Anything other than actually *teaching.* Therefore, there were often no signatures in the register. They would later be filled out by compliant colleagues. It was illegal to leave a class of underage students unattended for such long periods. The school principal knew this very well. At that time it was a national scandal, in which almost every school was complicit. There was always a story about some teacher or school being sued because of some incident that happened in class. I took the decision, almost frenziedly. In a mixture of thrill and anger, I photocopied the unsigned class log, convinced that one day it would come in handy. And I was right. Boy was I right...

I had already been warned that I would have to repeat the year. They didn't care about the problems at home. Since the school year was about to finish for the holidays, I decided that it was time to face the creepy principal, before it was too late. There was no way I was gonna repeat another day, let alone another year. She would have to grant me my requests. What other choice did she have? Besides, I had my delicious insurance with me. I felt no fear, as I stepped into her office. Seeing as I had nothing to lose, I casually put the evidence of the 'Crime' before her eyes. I had no idea how she was going to react, but I must admit the prospect *thrilled* me. When I finished talking, without betraying the whirl of emotions inside me, the principal smiled at me, but her face was as red as tomato. Her reply was smooth. She took in a deep, professional breath and composed herself.

"Never, in my whole career, have I been blackmailed. You have no idea what kind of hell you are diving head first into. Go back to class. I'll pretend none of this happened."

"It's not blackmail," I answered, with a private fire behind my eyes. "Let's call it a gentleman's agreement."

The principal took in some air, as she tried to penetrate my eyes and figure out this determined student in front of her.

"I'll decide what is best for this school," she answered dryly, with her Poker face.

I understood very well what that innuendo meant. A little tense, but amused, I left the room and returned to class. As I had hoped, the pressure made the principal commit a fatal mistake, which played in my favor. Mrs. Zelda rushed out of the office a few minutes later, carrying with her that very class log I had dropped onto her desk, in order to *fix* it. Naturally, I'd already made other copies, as extra insurance, or I would have surely found myself in shit so deep that I could have blown bubbles with my mouth.

My cunning trick was the key to my promotion. Everyone agreed that they were *mistaken*, and that I deserved to pass the year, but their clumsy attempts to cover 'the mistake' with signatures' was miserably shipwrecked. I'm not totally proud of how I behaved, but I think there was no other way.

A few days later, on the last day of school, Mrs. Zelda caught up with me in the corridor, in front of the bulletin board. "So… I hear you won't be repeating the year," she said. I couldn't help but reveal the triumphant smirk on my teenage lips. She leant forward and added, "You won this battle, Eva, but if you ever show your face at this school again, I'll be on your case every minute of every day, waiting for you to screw up," she quietly warned, in perfect mafia style. Despite the gracious smile, I knew that The Zelda would hold a grudge written in stone, and that I would have had a lot of headaches, had I decided to stay on at the school. Anyways, a persistent fight, with an experienced opponent, with the reputation of a former political activist, was, in those days, out of my league. That woman was a *real fighter,* after all, not one of those nobodies who are only good at bullying when they have the upper hand. I took that last meeting as a sign of destiny. It may seem strange, but Zelda remains one of the few adversaries in my troubled life, who I still admire and respect.

After the experience with my previous school I found it difficult to find my path, because I still didn't know what I wanted to do with my life. I drifted from one school to the next, staying no longer than a few months at a time. In the end, Mom, exhausted, forced me into a school of her own choice. A new school, a new life! This time it would be *different*. This time I would get along with the teachers. Or so we hoped.

Since this new school was considered a major league school in Vicenza, it would, Mom felt, suit my development. The new professors weren't any better. Even in this super VIP school, there was another bad apple; a professor whom we called Don Vittorio, who had the habit of preaching and whining about young, modern people; how they would never amount to anything in life, and would live on the backs of their parents forever. It was an unbearable attitude, but I didn't pay much attention to it at the time. I only thought of this sad, frustrated man, who could only unleash an utter inability to be charming and inspirational; a bitter man, angry for his own failures, still paying the price for his own disappointments. When we're young we don't immediately notice that we're surrounded by disillusioned and cynical people. We can't appreciate that they must have had opportunities, but allowed the machine to grind them down, and transform them into these flat, repressed, wounded creatures. If this was what the machine and the system did to people, I wanted no part in it.

So this Don Vittorio. One day in class, I had to back up a friend of mine, because he was taking more words than necessary to answer a question. I figured the right thing to do was to cover him. Without being encouraged, without raising my hand, I tried to explain to Don Vittorio, what my classmate was trying to say. It was an irresistible impulse, I admit, but the professor's reaction was totally hysterical. He began yelling at me, saying that if I wanted to talk, it would be better if my parents paid the fee on time (it was true, we were behind with a couple of instalments) and that a rookie like me had no right talking back to an adult.

He was like, "You have no respect...blah...it's a disgrace and an insult... blah...Do you know to whom you're speaking...blah...blah... Do you know what a privilege it is to attend such a reputable school? Blah, blah..." His face looked like a sweating beet, as I let him scream his lungs out. When he finished, I carefully got up from my desk and left in silence. There was no way in hell I would be wasting any more time in that spoiled and self-entitled institution. I later learned that poor Don Vittorio had almost collapsed to the ground from the stress of his outburst. Too bad his ego or his health couldn't take a hit from a so-called rookie.

Chapter 3

I DON'T KNOW IF IT was out of disgust or exhaustion, but I decided that I was done with student life, at least for the time being. Was it me who was outta place or was the whole world a sinking ship of fools? How could I tell? Enough was enough. I figured that if I went on like this for much longer, I'd probably wind up in an asylum.

In those days, finding a job wasn't difficult, especially for a hot girl. In no time I found a place to make some cash; some small ice cream shop downtown. It wasn't particularly a challenging job but it was enough to give me some downtime from my troubles. Not only did it give me an allowance, to appease my teen appetites, but it also helped me to chill. Nardo, as we called the owner, maybe sensing I was looking for some moral support, took me under his wing and treated me good. He was a patient and better teacher than most of the sour faces at school. Math was one example. On my first day, I wasn't even able to give the correct change to customers, and this was embarrassing, especially when some guy thought I was playing smart with the small change. Nardo's patience and kindness prevented me from going crazy during that time in my life. In that cozy shop I also met some of the most significant characters of my life, even if I couldn't imagine then how significant they would be. In the end, however, as my security grew, so did my needs. Working for Nardo was no longer enough to bring in the cash, to live the life I wanted.

I had some friends who used to organize these extravagant evenings at the local discos and clubs. These promoters were always on the lookout for some new talent with a fresh attitude. They knew that I was an uninhibited girl, who didn't have a problem dancing on the stage. They knew immediately, in fact, that behind my eyes existed a simmering passion. This was true. I've always carried a longing to escape and to express myself, and in doing so, would expose the deepest desires and pleasures of my audience, who would abandon themselves in my audacious and sensuous new world. It sure wasn't what my family dreamed of for my future, but in those days my attitude was kinda 'Screw it! Free entry and drinks! That'll do nicely!'

What struck me in no time was the fact that, probably because of my candid and sensual approach, I became more successful and *more requested* than most of the professional dancers, who frequented these venues. Teased and caressed by the lights, as the adrenaline pumped thru my pulsating body, dancing took me *closer to heaven*. Lost in the ecstatic disco beats and the euphoric rhythm of the night, my lustrous skin and chic outfits, swayed and moved in an everlasting neon-lit dream. In this inner sanctum, my incandescence was the center of *everything*. It was sure overwhelming and addictive hearing my name cried by the DJs and vocalists in these legendary venues in Vicenza. If fame was a drug, I was hooked big time. I wanted my name to be called at the Olympus! I promised myself that I would conquer the world of lights and music. It was my destiny.

During this phase of my life I made many friends and contacts. One such girl was Marjana, a classic Balkan beauty. With her opulent lips and stunning figure, she swaggered through those disco nights, like a modern Hollywood diva. She danced fabulously, and with her exotic traits, there was hardly a night where some horny chancer wouldn't try his luck with her. As she stepped onto the podium, and the DJ dropped the beats, the crowd would stare at her lips and her body, unleashed in a whirl of sweat and pheromones. Like my own experience, it was as if there was a *danger* to what she was doing. She wasn't just *dancing* but responding to the call of the primal *instinct*. Recognising that I possessed an enigmatic charm of my own, Marjana introduced me to a small local agent, who offered me a job in PR, in various fancy locations all around Italy. It wasn't the big living I was used to, and it wasn't quite the 'big time', but it wasn't so bad either.

Indeed, it was while dancing in the clubs around Lake Garda that I met my first love: Domenico, a pizza maker from Naples. He worked in a restaurant in Sirmione. Like most pizza makers, he had big dreams of escaping and making a name for himself. One time he came to Vicenza while my sweet granny was visiting relatives in Germany. I 'borrowed' the spare keys Mom left in case of emergency. It was the perfect opportunity to host my lover and see what he was really made of. Although I wasn't an expert, he was very tender, and helped me overcome the embarrassment of discovering my own body, right there, in my grandmother's bed; silhouettes exploring the shape of love, skin on skin. I feel like laughing now when I think about it, but I think my grandmother would have understood too, if she had seen the beautiful face of the Neapolitan I loved. Domenico was ambitious and intelligent. I followed him to his home in Secondigliano where I found charming, easy-going people, but I was too accustomed to Vicenza and to the Venetian mentality, so my first reaction was probably disoriented and stilted. The Neapolitan people are big, open, grandiose characters. They live their lives with grand gestures and strident voices. If you are befriended by a Neapolitan you have a friend for life. If you have a problem with anything, it only takes a phone call or a favor from a friend to set things straight. Wherever you go, anywhere in the world, once you've been to Naples, you carry the Neapolitan spirit with you forever. In Italy there's always been a rivalry, not just between the North and South, but amongst the regions. Northerners are considered by the South to be rigid and remote. Severe workaholics. There's an old joke that the tight-fisted people of Genoa are like the T-Rex: with short arms that can't reach their pockets. Those in the South, meanwhile, are considered by the North to be casual, friendly, cunning, rule-breakers, who live on the backs of the Northerners. When you see a group of quiet Neapolitans, the Northern mind wonders what scheme they are plotting. In Italy, *everyone* is suspicious. Everyone looks you directly in the eye. For a foreign visitor, the scrutiny and interest of the Italian can seem intense, but it's just our way of trying to figure out if we can trust you. Italy is still young. It only officially became a unified country in 1946. As with America, Italy is like a rebellious teenager that hates being told what to do by the so-called serious, responsible 'adult' countries, such as France, Germany and England.

In Naples, Domenico had stacks of big ideas but despite our starry-eyed plans, the status of our relationship was headed on a downwards spiral. It was difficult to pinpoint exactly what was happening to us, but perhaps he could sense I was homesick. He was always promising that as soon as he was established with his business, he would move North indefinitely. I had no reason to doubt him because I was crazy about him. As time went on however, I could see the division between his ideas and our reality. I couldn't fully adapt to this life, and felt constrained by our commitment to one another. Things were either rushing too fast or standing still. I thought back to how free I felt, during those disco nights in Vicenza, on that podium, under the lights, with the music transforming me into a *superhuman* temptress.

Something seemed to break in this apparent endless love, until we both understood, sadly, that there was no future for us together. It was simply the wrong place and wrong time, perhaps, with the wrong person. We often discover in the course of our lives that the 'right person' can be the 'wrong person', and vice versa. After all, life and love isn't as lucid as the romantic fictions. Domenico and I kept in contact. In fact he gave me a call some years later, half hysterical, because his life was falling apart and he couldn't see a way out. I calmly put him in contact with a friend who found him a job in Miami. Domenico moved in with my friend and worked like a dog for months, until he ended up becoming a gigolo for a wealthy heiress. That wasn't all. Once he had grown tired of the rich lady, he used the money he earned and started a cushy life in Monte Carlo, where he met and married the rich owner of a well-known local restaurant. It's funny when I think about it today. It's one thing having big ideas, and getting stuck in a quagmire, but we sometimes need the bold push or pull in the right direction from our honest friends, which can lead us to an amazing destiny, no-one could have expected. I am still grateful to Domenico for not dragging me into a complex soap opera that would have made us both unhappy. The best thing we did was to release each other, which is often the most compassionate thing you can do for somebody. Throw the cage open!

CHAPTER 4

I RETURNED TO THE SMALL ice cream shop in Vicenza, hoping that the familiar setting, with familiar faces, would reboot me, but something was missing. I was still aching for something I couldn't describe and the quality of my work was unfocused. As for my folks, Dad still couldn't land the funding he was counting on. The nightmare wasn't over. Knowing that I had to return home day after day, and face the farce of this existence, and feeling utterly useless to provide comfort to my brothers, undermined any remnant of goodwill I could grasp. Nothing had changed. The *bella figura* sure couldn't pay the bills.

The turning point came when I got to know two regular customers who often came into our shop, for coffee and gossip. They would often compliment me on my demeanour and my 'Lolita beauty'. Had they been guys I might have told the creeps to take a hike but these women immediately interested me. There was something different and *magnetic* about them, which attracted me in a platonic way. Their body language inferred an air of luxurious confidence that absorbed me. I wasn't to know, until later, that they were *escort girls*. In any case, whenever they came in, they made my day less tedious, with their kindness and curious tales. I observed that their interest in me was genuine.

One of them, the most striking in her looks, was nicknamed Milady. She was one of the best paid mistresses in northern Italy. At the beginning, some of her stories made me edgy and uncomfortable, but I soon understood that she wasn't trying to shock, scare or play games with me. She was being honest. Over time, however, the uneasiness faded and was refilled by a bourgeoning curiosity to hear more of her experiences.

In that bar we began to chat like long lost friends, about the incredible feats she had experienced. I eventually found her to be one of the few truly open-minded people I have ever met in my life. She opened my eyes to a world that I never knew existed, a sexual underworld, where desire and lust were often locked away behind rigid facades and private bedrooms. I was a girl from a good family. Everything I heard, with growing interest, aroused a hunger in me. A hunger for more information. A hunger to learn. A hunger to express myself in a more sensory fashion. Sexual passions, I learned, weren't only strange and sometimes painful but instinctive desires, and once we understand the various things men want, they can be played like an instrument. For example I remembered how Domenico was always so physically sensitive. Because of my lack of experience I didn't know at the time how to, shall we say, *handle* him right.

Milady and her companion enjoyed their work very much. Judging from her packed wallet, she would nonchalantly take out of her purse every time she needed to pay for something, I could see that her job was lavishly rewarded. The more she gossiped, the more I learned about the ways of the world and the ways of the human mind. For example I discovered that she was the lover of several business men in our vicinity, including many self-righteous, hypocritical defenders of the traditional family. Also there was a well-known businessman from the Middle East, perhaps even a trusted ambassador of the Sheikh of Oman, who was handling big business in Italy. He was one of Milady's best customers, so much so, that he often had problems with his regular wives, because he often gave much more expensive gifts to the dominatrix than to them.

Married guys aren't always satisfied with their wives. They can't pleasure or be pleasured by them. They don't talk about sex but the latest family ritual, the banking scandals or idiotic politicians. What they secretly crave is to be ridden (with bridles and a saddle) by Milady. They yearn to be dressed as a lollipop girl in stockings and to be verbally abused. They dream of having their noses crushed under the curvaceous butt of Madame's skintight breeches, begging for air. Their midnight fantasies involve leather, Spandex, masks, S&M, strap-ons and a twitching sensory craving for the associated tastes and aromas. Eye-contact is just as arousing to a man as moist lip pressure on their members. They long for this and the escorts provide the service, without the blue haze headache of Viagra.

Viagra is often for disappointed wives. If men and women truly, openly, revealed what they wanted and needed, and explored their fantasies, maybe there wouldn't be such a *vast* need for high-class pleasure girls and male escorts. Instead, as we have seen through history, escort girls are blamed for the delirious desires of the men, which are in fact *natural desires*, no matter how strange. Throughout history, escort girls have been hung out to dry by a mean-spirited, prudish believe system, and subjected to this abuse by *other women*, who haven't had their 360 degree passion, *unlocked*. Escort girls are often demeaned, not always by men, but by the moral bastions of sisterhood, who can't accept that many of the girls who provide this high-class service are in *control*, and make their own decisions. I'm not talking about poor girls, exploited by pimps and hooked on drugs, hanging around train stations, offering sad BJs to grotesque beasts; this indeed is criminal and must be stamped out.

I learned to love Milady. She had charm, charisma, glossed with a disturbing shade. Her personality was that of a dangerous predator: she knew all too well what she wanted, because she knew what men wanted, and didn't care about the way she would get it. Listening to her stories was a secret privilege. It elevated me higher than the ordinary people around me, because I had this special friend and they didn't. I've always been mesmerized by extraordinary people. Anyone who stirs my interest and revitalizes me is immediately welcome in my world. Over the years I've developed my gift for *instantaneously* recognising those with a dark heart, a burning, troubled spirit or an air of mystery. If I spot someone for a few seconds, and there's something that intrigues me about them, I can remember them forever. The mind often lies to us and denies who we are, but chemistry doesn't lie.

It was Milady who suggested that perhaps it was time for me to become more independent. I never went down that dark alley, however. To ride an entrepreneur or give a notary a steamy golden shower wasn't my jam. Whatever floats your boat, guys!

CHAPTER 5

MILADY'S FRIEND, SABRINA, WAS a beautiful, simple girl from Mestre, near Venice. She worked in the surrounding towns to avoid small-minded country talk that could upset her young children. Every now and then she worked as a Go-Go girl in the discos, being very attentive not to mix the two jobs. We would meet, without the intense, voluptuous presence of our mentor Milady. Caught between sympathy and awe for my natural beauty, she was more than happy to listen to my frustrations about the tiring situation at home. I had to make the break. I had to escape once and for all and make something of myself.

When I finally made up my mind, I grabbed my things and stole away. In just few hours I moved into her small and modest flat near the city center. We split the bills and I did my fair share of the housework. I also helped Sabrina keep track of her 'clients'. It wasn't a brothel as such. I guess, like many people, she was just working from home, providing a *friendly* service. No different to a car mechanic. Guys would come and explain their problem and she would work her magic, give them a *revisione*. Around us there lived some nice families and students of architecture, who rented the place because it was kind of old, thus cheap. Maybe they knew about Sabrina's games, but, if they did, they seemed totally indifferent. I'd be lying if I said that I felt at ease with her lifestyle. I couldn't help but hear the rapturous moans, filtered through the paper thin walls, between 11am and 1pm every day, knowing that Sabrina was *taking care* of seven or eight customers. I wondered if I had made the right choice moving in. Then again, every dark side had a bright side, and the fact of the matter was, tough as it sounds, I was free of my family.

As with Milady's clients, Sabrina's appointments were almost all respectable 'family' guys, well known professionals, lawyers and bankers, who often had the audacity to phone their bourgeois wives right there, in the hall, as they were patiently waiting for their turn, to explain that they would not be able to come home in time for lunch or dinner, because they were up to their necks in work. Yeah, right! I managed to get used to everything: the noises, the impossible hours at which I had to answer the door, to the smell of sweat and sex and the dirty stains in the bathroom. It's amazing how the mind is adaptable, and capable of finding something positive in every situation. After all, Sabrina's returning customers often left this *skin mechanic's* cushioned 'garage' satisfied.

Meanwhile, even though I was working between the kiosk and the apartment for more than half of the day, for the first time I felt that I had some kind of control over my destiny, which allowed me to mature further. I had lived too long in my cocoon. I was finally shaking the role of the blonde airhead out of my hair, whilst trying to preserve the dignity of my family. As much as I had tried to be a wholesome person, I had become stagnant. I couldn't hope for any real maturation if I betrayed who I was maturing into. I had much to offer. I learned to precisely observe what was happening around me and *aggressively* to change what I didn't like. It was a slow but fundamental process, and I soon realized that things were changing when I noticed that instead of looking just at my tits, people would stare into my eyes, whenever we talked. I had control. If anyone was going to control the direction of someone's eye-contact it would be me. Even Milady treated me as something more than a half-assed disciple. Her juicy grin of approval was the cherry on top of the cake of my victory. Had I finally matured into a young woman? I would like to say it was so, but the story was far from being over.

Sabrina, knowing her job only too well, treated her clients as if she were really in love with them, and more often than not she entertained them more than was needed. It annoyed me for the simple reason that those pigs took advantage of her body and lack of entrepreneurial cunning.

"I don't fucking care about customer loyalty, Sabrina! These horny chancers are fleecing you. You're worth more than you give them! You're supposed to be a business, offering the services *you decide*, for the price you decide," I told her one day. She gave me a blank stare. Milady's speeches had broadened my horizons. What was it that Sabrina wasn't getting?

"You can't let these deadbeats use you like some cheap, inflatable pleasure doll! These pests are nothing but pitiful Cassanovas who take their sweet time. All you get are worthless crumbs!" I flared. "You have to be more selective, if you want to get something out of this life. When are you going to realize that your time is your money? You have to refine your clients, cut your services, and raise your prices. If they don't like it they can go find some cheap mouth outside of Mestre Station to empty their balls into!"

I was surprised at how I was talking. Was this turbo-charged, feisty woman, the person I was becoming? It didn't sound like me all. But whatever had pushed me to say those things, I had Milady to thank for it. Sometimes people need to hear the things they don't want to hear, or they'll spend their whole lives as a doormat. From that moment, the quantity and quality of customers changed, and so did my living conditions. The change in my habits and the flow of far more respectable people, than the ones we were used to, allowed me not to get more involved in the network of gossips and basket cases that I seemed to attract in that place. Sabrina was changing too. She seemed happy and looked healthier than ever. She clearly had a renewed admiration for me. Although she never managed to convince me to become an escort, as she would have liked, we became much closer than I ever imagined. When the day was drawing to a close, if she didn't have to run to Mestre to see her children, we would spend the evenings together as good friends. Wonderful moments. For the first time in ages, when the whole world around me seemed like a brothel, often in the most literal sense, I felt like a normal person.

CHAPTER 6

M
Y LIFE HAD BECOME like a swing. I didn't want to totally
abandon my youth, my old friends and classmates. I secretly
wanted a regular and relaxed life like theirs, but I knew it was
no longer possible. They didn't know the unstable waters I was sailing
through. A friend suggested that I should do some temporary work at the
fair in Vicenza, famous for its marvelous gems and gold.

Working at the Vicenza Fair wasn't that rough. A few hours of work
a day could pocket me around 350-400 Euros a day, which at the time
was a pretty good snatch. Since this cash was earned with the sweat of
my forehead and cunning, and not between Sabrina's thighs, it gave me
more satisfaction. I got my kicks observing the distinguished businessmen,
strolling aimlessly from one stall to the next, expressing more interest in the
priceless cleavage and legs of the hostesses, rather than the merchandise.
To be honest, I never really fell under the spell of the fair. I was far more
interested in the possible business opportunities I could arrange with these
gents, than in the glitter of those splendid jewels. These horny devils could
be potential customers for my friend Sabrina, I thought.

Obviously I wasn't the only one making some spare cash at the fair.
There were high school graduates, as well as many professional hostesses,
who generally came from some of the shadiest agencies in the country
towns, not to mention the offspring of the bourgeoisie, all requested
by a compliant manager; a lady very well connected with management
of the fair. A couple of us were placed on the stall of this super spoiled
Turkish Daddy's boy, with his masculinity issues. At best he treated us with
undisguised contempt and at worst, like we were slaves.

I occupied my mind with false plans to rob him like the little bitch he was, or more simply, I imagined myself with a beautiful tiara on my head, looking like a princess. The idea of making business teased me more and more every day, so much so that I could hardly bear to see all these opportunities pass under my eyes, while I was busy dusting storefronts. The illustrious entrepreneurs gave me the inspiration. In the middle of a great market downturn, while almost all production from the Vicenza area was floundering, fairs were no longer a meeting place for weaving new business relationships, but a showcase of automatons with false shit eating grins, trying to convince others that they could still afford their trophy partners. Between gala dinners, after a couple of bottles of champagne, there were always those who couldn't resist the company of some beautiful woman. This Turkish asshole took full advantage of the occasion, calling me over to his stall as he pleased. With my shirt slightly unbuttoned, I sat nonchalantly next to the sitting duck of the day. The beautiful diamonds, along with my equally beautiful breasts were enough to convince most people that our stand deserved a second visit.

Out of the blue Milady appeared, to give me the boost I needed. I met her by chance, while I was having coffee. I couldn't have been happier to see her, a vision of elegance in the midst of chaos. The She-Dragon (another nickname I gave her) went around the fair with a vast assortment of jewelry: gifts from her customers, including a beautiful Royal Asscher cut straw diamond, a keepsake from a well-known lawyer. It wasn't the first time, partly due to her negotiating skills, partly thanks to the providential presence of the wife of the client, that my friend squeezed the fair.

The best deal she made was when a customer from Tel Aviv, who had entertained her during the previous fair, brought his wife with him that year. This presented Milady with the perfect opportunity to negotiate.

"Men, pff," she sighed, leaning close to me, eyeing her easy victim. "So predictable. You see that guy at the stand, on the right? That one with the blue kippah on his head? He may look like a rabbi, but I know for a fact that he adores having a champagne bottle shoved up his ass."

I couldn't help but laugh. That wasn't even the funniest part.

"The funny thing is that the 'champagne' was a knockoff, some cheap Venetian prosecco I picked up at a local convenience store!" she revealed. "Hm, his stall sure has some charming items. I wonder..."

"You're wicked!" I laughed complicity.

"Well wouldn't you just look at that! Aw, how devoted he is to his poor wife. Don't they make a sweet couple? Of course he's gay, but the poor thing doesn't have the courage to accept it."

I began to understand that something else was buzzing in her head, and that her references to Jews weren't just causal jokes. It made me uneasy to be honest.

"Watch and learn how simple it is," Milady purred. "I'll go there, sit my sweet ass down and let him serve me as a real lady. He'll be professional and courteous. As soon as his wife goes away, I'll choose the things I *really* like, and remind him about the special discount we *discussed* last time."

I was stunned. I couldn't believe she was actually going to go for it. She was playing hard ball. As I was about to ask about the *discount* she was referring to we were interrupted by the Turkish *first lady*, this ass-slapped Daddy's bitch who, although I was still way into my break, was almost sitting on my lap with an air of dispassion, tapping on his fake Rolex. He was always breathing down my neck. His total lack of manners was the last drop. Milady almost laughed when she saw me heading for the stall, probably anticipating a scene.

"Hey girl! It's a mess. Don't keep the customers waiting. You aren't paid to talk shit all day!" he whined. 'I got girls queueing all the way up to Trento for a gig like this.'

I eyed the jerk with a petrifying smile.

"Go fuck yourself!" I said.

I left him in the lurch, knowing I could lose my job, and that it wouldn't be easy to come back, if I ever needed to. We should never leave doors fully closed, but slightly ajar, in case we need to sneak back in. However, I made sure to keep my free pass, and decided that I would return to carry out my plan. Luck was once again on my side because, at the entrance, I met Stefano, a nice gentleman I had known during those days of slavery. He was about forty and had a great taste in fashion.

"What are you doing out here, beautiful?" he asked me. "What's up? No more work from Turkish cry baby?"

I explained what had happened. He laughed cheerfully. "In that case you can come to the gala dinner tonight, here at the fair. Here's my number. I won't take no for answer! Dress smart, if know what I mean. I'll send somebody to pick you up!"

His invitation raised my spirits. It was also an excellent opportunity to get to know more important people in the business world.

I arrived that night wearing my chic John Galliano red dress, a gift that I graced myself with the first gains in that world of courtesans. I saw giant crystal chandeliers above the tables and a riot of flowers and decorations. This is the place *I belong* to, I thought, not that dump of a home. I could never have brought Sabrina here. She might have been a sex machine, but she wasn't the right person for an event like this. She was too raw and ignorant, and it would have been immediately clear that she was an escort. Besides, I noticed that Sabrina was beginning to get envious of me, because I was the one being granted entry into a sophisticated world, she could only dream of. She stayed silent, but I knew she was jealous. What could she do? She needed the business I gave her.

That evening a man also approached me, with a glass of wine. We drank to our health. With his strong Anglo-Saxon accent, he announced that his name was Michael. He wasn't handsome as such, but full of charm. I discovered that he was a New Yorker of Jewish descent. We danced all night, and it was a pleasure to find such an exquisite person. For the first time in my life I felt a strong chemical reaction towards someone. I was totally rapt. I've never been one of those girls who are just attracted to classical beauty, or some brainless hunk. Mystery and mental stimulation have always been a huge turn on to me. This Michael looked like the devil; his intimate facial expressions and body movements, provoked and teased me. He had me in the palm his hand, so much so, that I had forgotten the reason why I was at this gala in the first place. I couldn't resist him. Within a few hours we were already at the hotel, playing our intimate night games, without a care about the world outside. The one night stand was another new experience for me.

I never expected that what I thought was merely the adventure of a single night, would last much longer. Before I even had time to reflect on what any of this meant, he was calling me from New York, promising to spirit me away. I'd always felt that someone with my ambition was wasted in this stone cold hole of a city. It was so easy letting fantasy give my illusions wings, because I wanted to escape from this venal, mercenary world, where pigs in Gucci, were still pigs.

I wanted to believe in Michael's good intentions.

This is why I waited patiently for the next fair. I had already found quite a few customers, but the most important thing was seeing him again. The few months that separated one fair to the next seemed like years.

I felt two hands covering my eyes. I immediately recognized the intense scent of his skin. "Michael!" I cried. As we kissed passionately, some of his Italian colleagues passed us, including my friend Stefano. It was a pleasant meeting, but part of my mind was focused on business. Michael kept the greeting short, so as not to arouse suspicions about our relationship. I found it incomprehensible when he asked me to keep it secret. He quickly scooted away, leaving me standing there with mixed emotions. Fortunately, my loyal Stefano, who had witnessed to the kiss, jogged over to me. He asked me if I had any idea what I was doing. I shrugged. What was the problem?

"You probably don't know this," he said, secretly amused, "but that guy's been married for years. Turns out he has three children."

I was dumbfounded. I didn't want to believe what I was hearing. Stefano's gaze was sincere. A simple question was enough to convince me of his concerns.

"Has he ever invited you to his house?" Stefano probed.

"He always talks about this beautiful hotel right across from Central Park," I reflected.

In that very moment, I realized what I was saying. Why would Michael invite me to a fucking hotel, when he owned a stylish penthouse in Manhattan? I felt that someone had smashed my heart to pieces. There I stood, in the midst of the fair, no longer aware of all those passing chancers, players and hypocrites; shopping for guilt gems for their wives. These assholes were cruising and window-shopping every moist pair of lips and every hot body in the vicinity. My initial disappointment gave way to a *dangerous desire* for revenge. While I never shed any tears, inside I roared like a Cheetah. So many confusing thoughts flooded my brain. Why play with people's feelings? What pleasure did it give this man, to lie sadistically? I wouldn't forget this. There would be a price to pay. I was awake. I had to gather myself and stay focused. I had already created a small team of glamorous colleagues and classy escorts; younger and more agreeable than Sabrina. So I swallowed my anger. I didn't want to spoil my whole day. Michael kept bombarding me with calls but I left them unanswered, until the end of the evening. Without a care in the world for his duplicity, he invited me to join him at his hotel. This jerk really believed that if he clicked his fingers, I'd come running. I coldly replied that I was indisposed. *Besides, I had to manage some new clients: a colorful group from Dubai.* Maybe I would spend the evening after with him. Maybe not. I was holding the cards now. *Losing* has never been in my vocabulary. I always play to win.

The next morning, I rushed to Milady's house, and told her everything I'd discovered about Michael. She laughed like a madwoman.

"My little one," she purred, "…they're all the same. Copycats. Tell the prick to fuck off!"

I was baffled by her reply. Wasn't it her, with all her elegance, who had gone to *sit on that sofa* to claim her special discount? Milady then went into one of her regular monologues about how men thought with their dicks and most women never used this weakness to their own *advantage*.

I didn't let her finish. I immediately asked:

"Do you have any of your BDSM stuff? A pair of handcuffs, a whip …"

Milady surprised, but smug as a cat, pulled a riding whip from Hermes out of her *special* drawer

"I'd rather have handcuffs," I said, feeling agitated but excited at the plans my mind was cooking up. It was sure getting hot up there.

Milady casually took out some cuffs.

"Look at these beauties! Even the poor cops in US don't have a pair like these. Anything else you need, dear? Whatever the fetish, I have the gear."

As she rummaged through some more things, I noticed a nostalgic glint in her eye, as her fingers brushed the various silk and leather delights.

'Every object in here, not forgetting my *playroom*, has a special memory," she said, unfurling a beautiful black silk band and caressing it. "I expect this should come in helpful," she smiled knowingly. I didn't care. I stuffed it in my purse with the other things. For the rest of the day I wore a secret smile at the thought that no-one else knew what treasures and treats my purse contained.

When the evening came, I took a taxi to the hotel, where Michael was waiting. In my mind, I had already decided how the night would go. My intention was to tease and provoke him, so that he understood that we were playing *my game*, and not his. He was waiting for me, naked, but for the bathrobe, that barely covered his boner. I immediately tore his robe off and violently pushed him onto the bed. He never realised I could be so dominant; he had been used to my sweet and innocent side. This aggressive version of me actually turned him on more. I pulled up my dress and jumped on him, still in my delicious panties, and let him penetrate me, despite the lace barrier. The king-sized bed creaked, as I pressed my hands on his chest and rode him like some crazy horse. Suddenly, whilst he was still in the zone, I climbed off him and went to my purse, where I took out the handcuffs and the silk band. I bit my lip playfully, as I cuffed him to the bed and stretched the silky blindfold over his eyes. I lowered myself back onto him and resumed this kinky game for a few minutes longer, letting him believe that we were in for an unforgettable evening of passion. When I was sure he was close to a happy ending, I abruptly stood up and grabbed my clothes.

"What are you doing? Where are you going? What do you have in store now?" he smirked, still bound and blindfolded. The poor darling thought I was still playing.

"Getting dressed," I said, calmly.

He laughed. Sure, you're getting dressed, he probably thought. I reckoned he had been picturing me in an array of erotic outfits. Perhaps he was expecting me to surprise him in a skin-tight satin corset and fishnet hose, or maybe he was imagining me in an all-in-one black spandex catsuit, complete with cat mask and whip. In a crude gesture I removed the blindfold, but not the handcuffs. When he saw me in my regular clothes, touching up my makeup, he realized it was no longer a bloody joke. "Hey, what the fuck are you doing? Are you crazy?" he cried out. I smiled darkly, as I placed my scheming ass on the corner of the bed. He begged me to remove the cuffs.

"Ask your wife and your three children to untie you," I replied dryly.

Suddenly, Michael didn't breathe another word. He'd realized by now that he had been cold busted. I left the keys of the handcuffs on the bedside table, while he stared at the ceiling, furious but silent. I closed the door behind me. I knew what I was up against. For the first time in my life, I felt that I was making my own decisions. To that end, I decided never to trust people so easily. Especially, the lying lazy words of men.

The following morning, knowing that I couldn't just pop up at the fair, I decided to stay at home and chill. Stefano warned me that Michael was hell-bent on reporting me to the cops for my sexy antics.

"Two can play at that game," I said. "If that bozo tries to get smart, I'll go to his wife. I have contacts."

"What contacts?" Stefano asked.

"The ones you will give me!"

CHAPTER 7

"**Y**ES! YOU HAVE THE perfect looks and posture."

Through one of the Milady's contacts, I met a professional photographer, who convinced me to leave behind what remained of my 'coyness', to pose for his camera. His interest in my face and body was purely aesthetic. He wasn't one of those wise guys with wandering hands who spend most of the session 'handling' the *merchandise*, instead of the camera. This guy treated me as if my body were a sculpture by Michelangelo. According to him, the light simply adored the natural shadow my cheekbones gave off. The lens of the camera picked out my soft, clear but determined eyes. My full lips, in natural light, were as red as fresh rose petals, while my toned body curved under impeccable skin. The camera loved me and the photographer taught me to fully appreciate my body as a gift of nature, so much so, that my portfolio included some *nature* shots.

After delivering the snaps to a trusted agent, I relaxed and enjoyed myself. Amongst the various jobs, disco nights and my savings, I was able to relish a few weeks of total leisure. After some pretty turbulent months, back there, it was great to be reminded of what fun felt like. I also needed a vacation. As luck would have it, Milady also needed a break. She asked if I wanted to accompany her on a tour of the places she already had her *pied-a-terre*, as we say, or 'feet on the ground'. Why not? I figured I could save some cash and have a great travelling companion.

For the first time, I was able to visit Monte Carlo and some other regions of Italy, previously unknown to me; enjoying the evenings in Milady's company who, free of commitments, showed me the elegant sights and exotic scenes of city life.

I didn't think I was diving head first into a new mess, until I received a phone call from a well-known politician. At first I thought it was a joke, but I remembered where I'd heard his voice...

Months before, Milady and I had been sitting by the sea in Monte Carlo, waiting for the Grand Prix to begin. It was a beautiful day, and people were relaxing, despite the frenzy of the event, that had the entire city running around with spice up its ass. While we were talking about the butt of the waiter, who'd brought us our aperitifs, a man approached the table and greeted my friend warmly. He didn't seem like her typical customer, but it was clear he knew her well. Milady, as she did with all men, kept a certain, professional distance. He spent a while chatting with us (several hours, in fact). When he took his leave, he insisted that I give him my number, which I didn't deny him, out of politeness, since he was kind enough to pay the bill for us. I didn't take it that seriously at the time. (How many times does a guy work himself up into a sweat, to take someone's number, but doesn't have the balls to actually call?) Anyway, I would eventually find out how serious this guy was and how mistaken it was to give him my number.

Meanwhile, I got on with my life. I'd been reflecting on some proposals for a few photo shoots in several parts of Italy, when on one late spring day, I thought I hit the lottery. I took a call from the editor of a famous television program, Mrs Maddalena. She said that she was searching for some fresh faces, to add some zest to her team. 'Fresh meat'. A burst of emotion, with the irresistible fascination for the showbiz world, didn't leave me space for thinking too much. I was kinda paranoid too, but after the life I had with Sabrina, and the shit I had seen, I thought 'fuck yeah'. I was *ready* to get my ass on the road and show Bell 'Italia what I was made of. Maddalena invited me to dinner but, *unexpectedly*, she didn't turn up.

Instead I found my 'dear friend', the politician Filippo, whom I had met in Monte Carlo with Milady, that crazy afternoon of the Grand Prix.

During the meeting, he did nothing but praise my looks, saying how I had the perfect assets for the small screen. With his knowledge and contacts, it wouldn't be difficult for me to enter the magic world of TV, he suggested. I could be anyone.

"Y-y-you could be like Velina on Striscia! Or the hostess for the great Carlo Conti! San Remo Music Festival!! Oh, the possibilities are endless," he babbled on, taking sneaky glances at my tits.

I let him talk. Obviously, I wasn't very convinced, but even if he had found me a job reading weather forecasts on *Channel Hellhole*, I would have been more than satisfied. From the little I heard, talking to some local starlets in the nightclubs, where I shook my ass for a living, I would still have earned decent money doing an interesting, honest job, where I'd meet people from all walks of life. It was a super tempting offer that I couldn't refuse. As expected, the old man began making a few side allusions to some so-called 'management costs' that I had to pay, for his assistance. I must admit, even though I was expecting it, and we were in the middle of a crowded room, I had to repress the instinct to ask someone for help.

There was something so slippery in that old guy that gave me the creeps. So I did the thing I thought was right, and with an apology, told him that it was not the right evening. When I got up to go get a taxi, he mumbled some apology, and to make things even, he offered to take me home.

Thanks to the wine and the lack of witnesses, once we were in his car, he became more aggressive. His hands slithered between my legs. I didn't even have a chance to reach for the door. He grabbed me violently by the hair, and pushed my head down towards his opened zipper, from which the junk already appeared as a full boner. In the end, exhausted and scared, I told him to stop and let me out. He actually stopped, not at the edge of the road, but in the ravine of a curve, in the middle of some recycling bins. He began to insinuate that a cheap squeak like me, that was a friend to people like Milady, shouldn't be so demure. It was useless playing games with him, he implied. I should feel *honored* that he was infatuated with me, he suggested. I had to think of all the advantages that this liaison would have brought me. After all, he inferred, being the lover of a politician brought *special benefits*, and not just in economic terms. According to him, this was my lucky break and I had to take advantage of his burning desire to have everything that was on offer.

"You have to play ball with me," he insisted. "I'll transform you into a sex bomb! You will have TV and cinema offers coming out of your ass! You will meet producers and directors, thanks to me! What have you got to lose? How else do you think those divas and dolls out there got where they are? You think they rubbed Aladdin's Lamp and made three fucking wishes? Get real!'

It was like making a pact with the devil. I was stuck. Most of all, I feared his possible reprisal to my refusal. With his contacts, who could tell what accident was waiting to happen? Sometimes, in our lives, we come face to face with the devil. We find ourselves in the darkness, with absolutely no light, but it's here in the darkness that we find ourselves and can find the light; as long as we believe that we, and the people we love, *are the light*. Then the darkness doesn't seem so bad.

It is not easy to understand what *real violence* against women means: I was forced to start a sloppy blowjob on him, with tears and his developing discharge running down my cheeks: why did I have to do this? I hated him to death. The weight of his arms on my head made my struggles to take his jack out of my mouth impossible. I wanted to cut it off with a bite, spit his bloody demon meat onto the roadside, but at that moment I vowed that sooner or later I would make him pay. Oh yes. There would be sweet revenge. I suddenly stopped in the middle of this sordid spit and polish. I wasn't that kind of woman. I mentioned something about the fact that this was neither the time, nor the place. I tried to reason with him, hoping that there was still something good in him, since he was old enough to be my father. It would be better if I wasn't pressured, I explained.

At that moment, fuelled by alcohol, he turned fierce, threatening to ruin me.

"I can nail a dozen like you for a penny, whenever I want! You might wanna think about that next time, before you leave some blue-balled bozo to finish himself off!"

In my heart, I knew there was no worse feeling than that of rejection, but I realized that he couldn't be calmed, so I got out of the car and left him to cool down, starting at a brisk pace without looking back.

CHAPTER 8

I WAS EXHAUSTED AND FURIOUS. If he had been kinder, I would have simply refused his offer and the scene would have died there and then. This emotional blackmail kept burning inside me. Filippo had intoxicated me with dreams, only to then shove his dick into my face, like it was my only ticket to reach them. I was scared, confused and alone. It seemed to me, that this once magical forest of my dreams, I had whiled away so many hours of pleasure, as a young girl, was no longer an enchanted paradise but a festering swamp, with its putrid tentacles, creeping and twisting all over my body, trying to drag me underground. I'd met bullies before, who couldn't keep their hands to themselves, but the wickedness of this man *exceeded* all boundaries.

Every single evening, before falling asleep, thousands of plans were buzzing inside my head but come the morning, I had forgotten them. Meantime, Sabrina was continuing her life with her clients, as if nothing had happened. I saw no reason to involve her in what I considered my own *war*. First of all, I immediately contacted a lawyer, of whom I had heard great things, when my father was at the top. Dad sure wasn't happy being my intermediary. With all the mess my family was already going through, the last thing he needed was seeing his baby mixed up in all kinds of trouble and scandal. It was difficult to convince Dad to get me a lawyer, even though he lived in the celebrated hills, near my village; kinda like a local Bel Air, where small town celebrities built their small villas.

The well-known lawyer, Cesare, sure knew his shit. He saw this case as an excellent opportunity to give further prestige to his career. He immediately gave me some pretty cool advice on how should I behave, if I wanted to have any chance of success.

"Here is everything you need to file a criminal complaint," he said. "No matter what the court thinks about sexual favors, there are still grounds for an accusation of violence, even if the relationship hasn't been consummated."

The bad experience had left me finding it difficult to trust *any* man, let alone a respected lawyer, so I never revealed if there had been violence, both psychological and physical by the predator. It was high-time for this victim to become the executioner. This situation was years before the Harvey Weinstein allegations that would rock Hollywood and lead to the #metoo movement.

"Is it not enough to shame and expose this pervert in front of everyone and force him to pay?" I asked.

Maybe I had been watching too many TV series but wasn't 'flagrante delicto' sufficient to start a legal act?

"Not without the testimony of an eye witness," said my lawyer. "Even if you make him confess, you could still face a probable accusation of slander. If we're swift and cunning we might be able to catch him off guard. We have to look at ways of forcing him to repeat what he said you. We need witnesses. It won't be easy!"

I was totally split in two, because, on the one hand, I felt like a poor victim, who had to defend myself from an experienced and powerful man, while on the other, I was motivated by an unwavering thirst for personal justice. Alone with my demons.

"Keep in mind," the lawyer advised, "...that this case will feel like a long, turbulent marriage, with ups and downs. Between the process, and the aftermath, which could last forever, we might still be here when my hair turns white!"

I laughed at the joke, which at first seemed like silly (although in the coming years I understood very well what he meant). All I could ask myself was: why? Why had it come to this? Why do women always have to take this shit? Why is it that we're always treated as victims or alluring witches? After all, I had only wanted to meet someone who would guide me; a father, a life coach, a kind friend. Not a fricking serial blackmailer! The more I thought about it, the more pissed I was. In Italy the law protects men more than women, especially married men. Violence against women, especially married women, are often ignored by the police and courts, as they are *private marital* matters. Italian women have had to learn how to cover up their bruises, or stay indoors and do what they are told, for fear of more abuse. It may be the 21st Century, but the attitudes in Italian society, in many ways, is closer to 1970. As for other regions around the world, things are still the dark ages, in terms of equality and human dignity.

The lawyer filed my complaint and sent it to the offices of the courts. Perhaps it went somewhere beyond. Say, into the ears of a famous journalist, with connections all over Italy?

CHAPTER 9

"HI, CAN I SPEAK to the great madam, who reported a particular politician for a particular alleged sexual harassment?"

I thought it was a bad joke. I was about to slam the phone down, when a thought flashed through my head. 'Where did you get my number?' I certainly wasn't in the habit of scrawling my number on toilet walls in roadside restaurants. I was on edge. This wasn't the phone call I was expecting.

"Relax! I'm not an anonymous kidnapper! At least not at the moment! Hahahahaha!"

From the ironic tone, it was it was the kind of voice you could imagine being full of emojis, had it been a written on WhatsApp.

"What would you say, if we met at a place of your choice, and I offered you a shoulder to cry on… and maybe… a nice plate of dumplings?"

"You wanna tell me who you are, first?" I asked.

'It's a secret! No! Maybe! Say please, please!' the voice squeaked.

'Okay, I'm gonna end the call now,' I said.

We were walking on the fine line between the surreal and the unsettling. I felt cornered. On the other side of the phone was the sound of a cough.

"Peace, peace! Sorry, but I have a funny way of expressing myself. I tend to forget myself. Let's just say I'm a person who has their own reasons for wanting to see that guy in the slammer. I've built up quite a collection of rumors about his activities, but so far, no-one has had the courage to testify against him. Think you're angry and hungry enough to do it?"

"Only if you finally manage to string two words together, and tell me who the hell you are," I replied.

"Ivan Tomei! I'm a freelance journalist, always in search of the truth, however uncomfortable and hidden. No job is too big nor too small! No idiot is too stupid, or too tall! You like my presentation?"

I already liked him, even though I didn't know if I could trust him. An ally was an ally. I accepted his invitation to La Rivella, for some gnocchi with meat sauce.

From his voice on the phone, I imagined him to be much younger, but he was over forty. He looked a bit like Inspector Gadget, with this camel coat, from which at any moment, a tape recorder or a hammer could have appeared.

"Yeah! I understand why you drove our man absolutely insane! Wow!" he began. But seeing my expression, he changed the tone completely, and immediately became super professional. Between us, a plate of gnocchi and a platter of cold cuts, was an instant rapport. We got to work.

He put a computer in front of me, and on the display, brought up a series of dossiers. From the outside, we must have resembled two university students, diligently preparing a degree thesis, but the material I combed through was anything but innocent. I slowly began to realize what troubled water I was wading through: drugs, prostitution (including, allegedly, underage) and money laundering. This was hardly a pleasant profile to show off to friends. Ivan, on the other hand, didn't seem at all fussed. I wondered if it would have been better to leave the restaurant and forget about the whole thing. This crazy shit wasn't the kinda world I signed up for. What the fuck was I getting mixed up in?

"I won't lie to you," 'Inspector Gadget' cautioned. "This guy can really give us a bad headache." Ivan casually took a sip of coffee. "Not exactly mafia style, but not far off either. He's a useful idiot for some pretty dangerous people. It won't take them long to drop this Dumbo, if a mess should blow up."

Ivan made everything sound so easy. From what I knew, he could sure take care of himself in the underworld. I wondered what would have happened had I introduced him to Milady, but I soon dismissed that thought. My friend loved her freedom and privacy. She would have made a scene, like some crazy Mexican drama, if I got her tangled up into this web.

A few days later, Ivan introduced me to the rest of the team. Sebastian was strange but likeable. Argentine, was geeky and loyal. He took care of the technical side of things, such as wiretapping, hidden cameras, etc. He was young and passionate; just what we needed in this team, which had to be united for the coming battle. We also hired a private eye, who enjoyed playing the role of the handsome brooder, but also had an irresistible charm. He had that 'I wish I were Kevin Costner' groove that made every woman horny, including me. He latched onto Ivan and the geek because he could sniff out some 'heist'. They had already worked together, but so far they had only busted some managers living the high life with taxpayers cash, and a small time cheating drama, which ended in a tragic femicide. Maybe this was the reason he was protective of me. I really liked 'Kevin Costner'. I often fantasized about what we could do together, once the 'heist' was over. I don't know for sure what he thought of me at the time, but I think, in some way, he reciprocated my feelings.

Ivan called me a few days later. He'd gathered enough material to create dirt on our man, but he needed definitive proof. Was I still willing to act as bait? I confirmed my complete availability. Fortunately, I hadn't completely cut ties with that old pig. Playing on his vanity and narcissism, it wasn't that difficult leading that sleazebag into my trap.

CHAPTER 10

H IS VOICE ON THE other end of the phone line didn't have a welcoming tone. His pride still burned hard and bad, but I guess he wasn't the kinda guy to say no to an offer most men couldn't refuse.

"I just needed more time to loosen up," I began, when I realized that he had finally cooled off. "Listen, I was wrong. You just took me by surprise. You didn't have to be so aggressive. I was a shy, a bit afraid, you know?"

My words had to tease his imagination. I had to be slippery and persuasive.

"I'm sure we could, you know, make it up somehow. I'm really not so timid when the heat's turned up, yeah?" I lied.

Filippo blahed blahed and said that I still had a lot to learn. (Yeah, whatever) As long as I accepted another invitation, he was prepared to forgive me and give me a second chance. He already had clear ideas about how the evening should finish. He chose a bar near his home, with the not very subtle intention of oiling me with two Negroni cocktails, before immediately going somewhere for 'good gymnastic' practice. It was up to me to make him talk, or I could kiss my sorry ass goodbye.

Now I had to wait for the team. Alone in the hotel. It didn't matter how confident and prepared I was. With all this time on my hands, I had to remain focused and not think too much about what could go wrong. I couldn't lose control now. I couldn't give up, take the train back home and betray everything I believed in and those who had put their faith in me. It wasn't just Ivan's neck on the block or, for that matter, mine, but *every girl* down on her luck, with big ideas and stars in their eyes; rich pickings for scum like Filippo…

Let's pause and reflect. I suppose some of you reading this are wondering how I could have been so naïve. You're probably thinking: "Why did you get involved with that creep? You must have known that he only wanted *one thing* from you!" This is a typical opinion that too many Italians share when it comes to violence against women. They have little or no sympathy for the victims; not just the men, but the boring, old, frustrated, wives. They think we deserve this shit. They'll forgive their husbands, go back to their scratch cards and blame the innocent. They'll do anything to bury people like me, because they don't want to know the truth. Walking around Italy today are hundreds of Harvey Weinsteins. Fuck the haters. Or as we say in Italy: *Vaffanculo!*

We have to remember that I was barely out of college. I still had some growing up to do. One of the reasons I wrote this book, was to discover who I am and what it is that I'm searching for. Sometimes, we have to look back in order to look forward. Obstacles are placed in our path; that we have to overcome. Perhaps I'm searching for attention, respect, thrills, revenge, truth, justice, peace, fame, love and pleasure. What's your poison? I can be whoever you want me to be. I can be classy, I can be trashy. I can be sassy and chic. I can be funny and profound. How do you want it served? I can be who you want me to be, but *who am I?* Very often, in our lives, we walk into a situation, *knowing* it to be a trap. We know of the dangers and yet we still go ahead. The journey seduces us, and we are happy, at the time, to be seduced. But why? I guess I'm still asking questions. It's only recently that I can sense that I'm getting closer to the answer. There are days where I sure wish I could go back in time, give myself a hard shake and say, "What's gotten into you?"

… I went out, reluctantly from the hotel, and got into the car with the team, where we headed to our destination. I mentally reviewed everything I had to do and say. Maybe it was the adrenaline, maybe a renewed focus, but I started to feel a new energy that I never knew I had. It was as if I had been joined by a silent but benevolent presence. At the same time, this whole mess was farcical. If Dad hadn't lost control of the business, I might have wound up somewhere nice with him, with loyal, dependable friends and an honest guy, living a regular, wholesome life. Living *La dolce vita.*

The calm energy growing inside me suggested that it was just a way to try and justify myself, and to rationalize the chaos around me. Blaming my father and the unfortunate events of life was utterly ridiculous and pointless.

I stumbled as I got out of the car. The scene was so idiotic that I found myself laughing out loud. It was a hysterical laugh, dictated by stress and the need to release tension. People around me must have thought I was nuts, since I laughed all the way to the restaurant. In a strange way it was liberating. Sebastian planted some mics and hidden cameras in my bag and on my dress. He really cared about the success of the project. I listened for the hundredth time how to use the hidden camera and microphones; to be sure I wouldn't miss a single move.

I chatted with my small group of 'secret agents', hidden in the car, via the hidden microphones. My agents advised me not think too much and to remember our game plan and everything we had discussed. Now wasn't the time to let doubt creep in. When I saw the old fart approaching, with his slimy smile, every hesitation disappeared from my thoughts. This *motherfucker* was my Moby Dick, and this was the occasion to catch him and reel him in. Already a hundred yards away, I could feel his spine-chilling gaze and his predatory instinct. He threw himself at me, with the excuse of saying 'Hi'. I politely but smartly redirected his hands, in case they wandered under my jacket, and discovered my secret weapon. The loser thought he had me in his palm. Excellent start, I thought, but it wasn't enough to corner him. An old pig getting too touchy-feely wasn't exactly big headline news in a place like this. Fortunately, neither did the old man try and hit on me in the street, on our way to the bar. Dinner was nothing more than a formality for this brute. Strangely, for a guy who bragged about nailing a different woman every night, he remained as hungry as a college student. He was also as eager and unrestrained. I encouraged him by playing innocent. The more time we spent talking, the more juice we would have. Would any reasonable jury, after ninety minutes of shameless innuendos, consider our rendezvous to be an innocent game? In between mouthfuls of food, the jerk couldn't stop leering at my tits and slobbering about the great projects and plans he had for me. As long as I followed, to the letter, his orders, I could expect to have fantastic career in show business. He had already finished the second course, while my starters, only half-eaten, cooled on the plate. In the midst of all his promises, a minute barely passed where he wasn't gabbling about how hot I was, how mouth-watering my ass and tits were, how I was teasing him and how he couldn't wait to bone me into next week. I tried to stay on guard, as much as possible, with the firm intention to bust the fucker. Until now, he was being too 'civilized' by letting me take the reins.

"I'm still not convinced it's the right thing to do," I said, trying to look childish and lost. "Don't misunderstand me. I like being wooed. Really! This place is beautiful and the food is delicious, but you're putting too much pressure on me. Softly, softly."

He exploded all at once.

"Who the fuck do you think you are, bitch! You think I have time to waste with a prick-teaser like you? You either do as I say, or you can forget the star system! I'll cut your legs, you know that? I have a list of young girls, just like you, who can't wait to take a ride in Daddy's car. They'll do it just to please me or anyone who promises them a fucking spot in this shitty world. You understand? At least with me you'll get something cushy. If you prefer, go back to your shit hole and get banged for a couple of mojitos!"

He growled with a nastiness I didn't think was possible. He wasn't just belching some toxic masculinity but trying to break my spirit; pushing me to accept his advances. I had no words to describe the disgust I felt at that moment. Luckily for me, he dropped his guard and, totally unhinged, began to sing. He blurted out how he had power of life over death, and over the destinies and projects of those around him. One by one, he spat out the names of all the women who had 'been kind' to him and his friends, to get a spot on TV. He started to spill the beans 'bout how all the various wholesome girls hadn't been chosen for their skills, but because they had got down on their knees for a wide range of entrepreneurs and mafia guys. The *girl next door* was a fucking myth, said Filippo. According to him, these wholesome girls on TV, were nothing but slop, only good enough for the docile public, watching shitty, mind-numbing afternoon TV shows. If only you knew, he told me, how many sopranos and Miss Girls really launched their professional lives! They were real escorts, who got their 'virginity' back by dating the right guy (almost always, the customer with the fullest wallet). If I knew what was good for me, he told me, I would launch my career in the same way.

I was lucky to have met him, he said, not some cheap talent scout, who often traded women like cards, and left some poor losers, having achieved nothing, under the bridge; their arms often full of cocaine scars. He was still in mid flow, when, after getting the whole thing on tape, the team came to my rescue. I'll never forget the expression on his face, when he realized what was happening. I couldn't see how he expected to get out of this mess unscathed. The creep indignantly promised fire and fury to all of us; which would have scared anyone who wasn't used to such violence.

Fortunately, my new friends were calm and professional. Sebastian was enjoying the show slyly, as if it were just another scene he had already seen thousands of times. From the satisfaction on his face, I wondered if that was the only decent part of the job for him. The whole drama had been so surreal, and when we were all safely out the front door, I fell into Sebastian's arms and cried.

An hour later I vomited what I had managed to eat.

The complaint was sent in a timely manner, forestalling the article Ivan was writing by twenty-four hours. I found myself almost teleported in a flash to Cesare's office, with Senator Filippo's lawyer, who was trying to save face by shoving his nose so far up my asshole, I could feel it tingling. He begged, like a cuck, for my understanding. What could I expect from an elderly gentleman who had drunk way too much and so on? If I believed that the pig's lawyer was aware of the client he was defending, I would have spat in his face.

"It doesn't work that way," my lawyer said. "Our professional ethics decrees that we can't refuse a case, unless there is irrefutable evidence of our client's guilt. In such cases, we would simply refuse to aid and abet. But this doesn't happen often. Unfortunately, with the gains and rewards in our profession, you often get some unscrupulous lawyers botching a job and creating even bigger scandals."

When the Senator's lawyer left, Ivan and 'Kevin Costner' burst into the room.

"Here we go! The Carabinieri already have tried to seize the material. I'm gonna receive a warning soon. It's a badge of honour in my work. It can even kick open a few doors, but I don't think we saved the world."

As much as it bothered me, I knew the lawyers were agreeing for a conspicuous compensation, in exchange for my silence. Nothing but rubbish. I told them so. They all laughed.

"Ah, don't worry about that!" said 'Kevin Costner.' "As far as his friends in high places are concerned, he's a disgraced nobody now. He's damaged goods. Besides, if I heard correctly, your compensation will be pretty decent. Socially, Filippo is toast! You just wait and see! His life won't be the same anymore!"

I was frustrated. I demanded immediate results. My fist slammed the table.

"But I want to see him fall! Him and all his cronies! You have all this evidence. What's stopping you? Come on!"

"We've won the battle but we'll never win the war," Costner explained. "Our mission, more than anything else, is to *prevent* them from advancing. It's a never-ending story. A few heads will roll, but the big ones will always land on their shoulders. They'll continue to keep their cushy lives. We'll never know who they really are."

In some small way, however, I was very satisfied with the result. I don't know how the investigation had stirred the waters, but someone at the very top sure knew how to speed up operations, linked to the juice I had on our Senator. I didn't know how many people were involved or how important they were. All I knew was that there had been several searches in Rome, Florence, Turin and Naples, and several smaller towns. According to what Costner told me, there had been a lot of child prostitution and trafficking, which had now been eradicated. This was only the tip of the iceberg. Meanwhile, quite a lot of pimps and shady businessmen had been put in jail, and they would never again be able to harm anyone. I became worried about what the criminal underworld would have in store for me, if they knew the part I had played in the Senator's downfall. This was also the time when the infamous 'bunga, bunga' parties were breaking out. I feared that the domino effect of Berlusconi's scandals would eventually shine a light on my own case, resulting in me paying a higher price than I could have ever imagined. In Italy, accidents tend to happen all the time; especially to the innocent. The team supported me in its own way, laughing at me.

"We told you, business risk!" Costner laughed. "If they ever did something to you, it would prove that we got too close. In that case, instead of getting rid of dry branches, they would rally round and burn some witches in the square, while the devil laughs behind the curtains."

Flash-forward to March, 2019. Google the beautiful and magnetic, Imane Fadil; one of the alleged attendees of the so-called 'bunga, bunga' parties. Shortly after being admitted to a hospital in Milan, in early 2019, complaining of stomach pains, she died. She was just 33 years old. Prior to her premature death, she suspected that she had been poisoned.

CHAPTER 11

I IMAGINED THAT I WAS like the mythological figure, Hippolyta, Queen of Amazons; the heroine who would give women their due place in this masochistic society, not prone to selling their body for a show on TV. One day I discovered my sister in front of the screen, watching a local broadcast, trying to process the hot topic of the day.

Guess what the main item was? A sweet story about the black sheep, that our dignified city had given birth to; a self-centred girl of *dubious* morality, who, instead of working her ass off in some boring office and feathering her nest with an ordinary family, had decided to promote herself, at the expense of some 'respectable' family guy. Yes, it was *yours truly*; that shameless girl, whose buttocks were being slammed into the faces of thousands, during primetime, while respectable families were trying to digest their evening meal. Great result, I thought sardonically. (But I was kinda thrilled too). It felt cathartic, having the chance to talk about my experiences, and to express my righteous, unbridled anger in front of everyone, rather than keeping quiet for fear of being judged.

My sister's voice was plaintive and childish.

"What are you doing on TV?"

She was about twelve, and couldn't understand why big sis was on TV, talking about virile pigs.

"What did you do? Why are people so mean?" she innocently asked.

I tried to carefully explain.

"Listen, I didn't do anything I'm ashamed of, quite the opposite. I just told the truth about a mean guy, who tried to hurt me and failed. He won't be hurting anyone again. Now his friends are trying to bully me. Don't you remember? Just like school."

She remained silent with a sad appearance.

How could she understand? For her, television was the quiet space, where she watched cartoons and shows; safe adventures with happy endings; not a place where her sister's ass was on show for everyone to stare at. I realised there and then, that out there existed another world that was more dangerous for girls than boys, a place that would take your innocence and corrupt you in the shortest time. It sure wasn't a place for girls of my age, let alone young girls like her. She hadn't seen the world I had seen, naturally, but maybe she had already seen enough. I couldn't take the lost look she gave me out of my mind.

I left the house, slamming the door behind me. I felt lost. In my home. In my city. I needed some air, some space, someone to comfort me, anyone. Someone to tell me it would be alright, that this nightmare would end. Someone to *hold me.* Wherever I turned, people were ignoring, or pretending to ignore me. They were window-shopping, posing and talking shit; just the same old regular things the zombies in my city do every day. While Vicenza is beautiful city, with some genuinely fascinating and friendly people, it also has a reputation, like most of Veneto, of being cold and indifferent. In Vicenza, people live their lives as regular as clockwork. They're so encased in routine that they've lost the desire to be different. Instead they copy each other's routines and tastes. There's no passion here, only dispassion. They're all so fake and rigid. All these people ever seem to care about is tottering and prancing about in the latest fashions, whenever the new season comes along. You often have to *escape* from Vicenza to find any semblance of real life, creativity, fun and imagination. For a girl like me, who has always *flourished* on a diet of fantasy and lust for life, this place feels more like a penitentiary, than a prosperous city. I've always detested being ignored, like I'm a *nobody.* I'd rather have people staring at me and giving me verbal abuse than this...silence. Not one person gave a single, silent fuck. It was as if I had become *invisible.* I didn't know if they were afraid or embarrassed. After everything I'd been through, and all the effort I put in, the best I could hope for was to have these vultures gossiping *behind my back,* until they got bored when a juicier carcass came along. What the fuck was wrong with people? Not one motherfucker that evening, stopped to say 'Brava!' Or even 'fuck you!' Nothing. Zilch. *Niente!*

Something inside me broke. Perhaps it was my whole life crashing on my shoulders. I fell to my knees, at the edge of the sidewalk, with my head in my hands. I tried in vain not to burst into tears.

CHAPTER 12

A LTHOUGH THE SENATOR'S GOOD name would now always be tainted with shame and guilt, I didn't see this case as a victory. That man had, ultimately, gotten his way, while all I got in return, wasn't justice, but a wad of cash. Sure, it wasn't anything to sniff at, since it was a lot of money, but heck, I busted my ass trying to get that pervert in front a judge.

I was the only one in a bad mood by the time we left the room, after collecting my compensation. From the faces of the others, you would have thought we had won the lottery or hit the jackpot in Vegas. Still, I had to thank them. As an incentive, the Senator's attorney made a generous *contribution* toward my team's important *service*. Call it what you want. I call it 'wiping the client's ass.' Just crumbs, I thought, but they were happy with what they got. After repaying some small debts and helping Mom and Dad with some cash, there wasn't much left over to become a big shot in the stock market. Instead, I decided that it was time to invest in something closer to home: *me*. Since I wasn't particularly academic, I had to assert myself in other ways, to become the top dog.

In those days, poor Sabrina, evidently moved by a *jealousy* that had been brewing ever since I stopped inviting her to all those classy clubs, contacted some illiterate, sleazy 'journalists', who made a living spreading shameless gossip. She told them about all the ups and downs in my life, including the personal situation with my family. Out of *resentment*, I guess, Sabrina presented me to the local and national press, as a young careerist and charmer; a social climber and an It-girl, who targeted respectable professionals for cheap fame and money. What fame, I wondered? This was outta line because I did what I had to, not for myself but to try and save other girls from the hard destiny showbiz offers to screwed up kids. Whether it was to redeem the politician's reputation, or to shift a few copies more, who knew, but those tabloid dust rags didn't limit themselves to 'puff pieces' about my adventures. They triggered a full-scale media campaign against my character and name. There was something almost feral in the way they were mad at me and those that had helped me. Everything I did was purposely twisted and put in a bad light, with all the crazy, logic of a surrealist movie. If I stepped out for work or leisure, it meant I was clearly escaping from my moral responsibilities. If I dated a man, he was apparently the next unsuspecting victim on my hit list, or an accomplice for my next swoop. I couldn't wipe my own ass, without it being plastered on a sandwich board outside the newsagent's. To these scavengers, I was the flame-haired blond; nothing more than a common dangerous witch, who deserved to be burnt at the stake. Still, it didn't stop the paparazzi offering my pics to their failing publications.

If you imagine Vicenza as a bubble of ignorance and hypocrisy, then, to these witch hunters, I represent a sharp needle, ready to burst their bubble and let the truth leak out. What they wanted, and are still trying to do, is to blunt that needle. To this day, I'm still angry at those who judge me. Interestingly, such people, like *most people*, continue to lead their own sordid double-lives. Like they don't have phones with a dual SIM slot, for private conversations! Like all these respectable husbands never jerk to porn in the early hours of the morning, while their wives and kids are safely tucked up in bed! Like they aren't concealing some gambling or drug addiction! I don't care what people get up to. It's the hypocrisy I can't stand. This resentment of theirs is down to pure envy. How we all desire to be open and to be accepted. I've always been open about everything. I can't be shocked. I've seen the *other side*. Try me. There's a very famous and recent Italian movie called Perfect Strangers, which highlights exactly the stuff I'm talking about. Almost every Italian I know can relate to the themes in that movie. You can understand why we are suspicious. I believe the solution is to be honest and open, not closed.

Whether from out of cynicism or a darker reason, it was the first moment I seriously thought about giving up. Not only had I acted in a totally legit way, but I had also busted a filthy man. And I was the bad guy now!? I wouldn't have resisted too, if it hadn't been for the support of those who had accompanied me during some tricky situations, and the letters of solidarity I received from the well-wishers; able to see beyond the murk; where certain characters are used to dipping their pens.

CHAPTER 13

THE PHONE RANG. On the other line was the clear voice of Antonello Venditti. This guy was a journalist and an author with an interest in Italian politics not, he explained, *Antonello Venditti*, the famous Italian singer.

He said that my story had interested many people. His team had asked him to consider interviewing me, to understand if I was suitable for a national prime time show. He casually told me that we could arrange something whenever I liked. No rush. No pressure. I guess he imagined that I was on edge. After consulting my lawyer and feeling satisfied that there weren't any risks, I accepted the proposal. Fortunately, it was a harmless interview. I hadn't walked into an ambush with scandalous or leading questions. While I still felt nervous afterwards, I realised that it was the way a real interview should be conducted; with respect and decency. I promised myself that in the future, if one of Venditti's colleagues called me, then I would be sure to include him in the project. I've always believed that professional and honest people should be rewarded. To this day, I'm not ashamed of helping those with talent, a strong voice and message to share. When we recognise those with talent, we should water that talent and help it to blossom. I'm fortunate to be in a position where I can, at least, help people get on the ladder in the industry, be it in music, fashion and literature. I don't ask for or expect anything in return. Helping others is its own reward. As I often say: *Chiamami! Parliamo!* (Call me! Let's talk!)

Anyway, I got another call. I had to take a little breath to understand that, on the other end of the line, was none other than Maurizio Costanzo. For English-speaking readers, who may be unfamiliar with Costanzo, he is a famous journalist and film director. He's recently better known as the host of the longest-running talk show in Italy: *The Maurizio Costanzo Show*. Intrigued by my story, and recommended by Venditti, he invited me for a meeting in Parioli, Rome, to discuss my story. His show had big ratings and could launch careers. It would have been perfect! I was almost about to leave home without even packing. This was finally the opportunity I had been waiting for, to spread and share my message of revolt against this perverse system. This time, it was my lawyer Cesare telling me to relax a little. He helped me to dispel any last doubts and worries I had, about sharing my story. It was good, having him at my side.

Not even the sly beauty of Rome could take my mind off the physical discomfort I felt while reading and rehearsing my lines. While I wasn't in any danger, I was a little nervous.

"Mr. Costanzo is always extremely busy," Venditti told me, as I followed him into the presenter's office, and waited for Costanzo to call us in. Eventually, I found myself in front of him, this super famous man, I had seen on TV from my youth. For a while he seemed more interested in the piles of paper before him, than some hot but determined girl from Vicenza, hungry to smash the sexist system. I couldn't tell if he were actually reading or pretending to read. He looked like a small town professor, waiting to hear for the hundredth time why student Rossi had failed to do his Latin homework. Every now and then he threw me a side glace, which at times seemed to say: "Who the hell is this? What is she doing in my office? What is she doing out of class!"

As it turned out, Mr. Costanzo was nice, open and genuine. It was a pleasure talking to him. He took me seriously and treated me like a person, not a pair of tits. We discussed everything, my life, what I wanted to achieve, and what a career in television could offer me. Finally, he stared at me with his little eyes for a long time.

"Let me level with you. You're quite a smart ass! I can see it in your eyes. But you're also are a decent person. And that's the problem. If I put you on TV, the others would eat you for breakfast! You ain't powerful or famous enough yet to handle yourself. You're just not ready."

I started to object, but Venditti was faster.

"He's right, Eva. You don't know how things work on TV. People don't watch talk shows to see what's accurate, they just wanna see blood. It's like the colosseum, a few blocks away. Viewers want to see someone thrown to the tigers, see if they survive. Even with a classy show like ours. Mrs Average out there, watching TV, after a hard day, just wants to see you in a catfight with Maria Grazia Cucinotta. Even better if we get a boob flash in the process. If its culture they want, they can go watch Cecchi Paone. I guess if this were America, you'd be looking at chatting to someone like *Oprah*. But even then you need more experience on your shoulders and something to sell, understand?"

I couldn't hide my disappointment.

"No, don't be like that," said Costanzo, softly. "We can't choose the public. We can make the best show on earth, and hope that its quality will stand out, but make no mistake, the audience rules. If our show doesn't interest them, they switch off. And if they switch off, that affects sponsors and commercials. TV is a business. It's just a game and I've been playing it for a long time. Trust me. Look! You're still nervous. Take it from me, you're too young."

Somewhere inside, I found some courage.

"So what do you suggest I do? Why bother asking me to come here?" I asked, a little disappointed, but knowing in my heart they were right. Costanzo looked at me and smiled.

"Eva, you're nice, beautiful and dynamic. Your moment will come, believe me. Go to the Trevi Fountain and toss a coin in! Go eat pizza! Go to a disco! Be young and foolish! Do you really need me to tell you what to do with your life? As far as I can see, you've already got this crazy world worked out," Costanzo said.

As I got up to leave, he stopped me. "In fact, why don't you write a book?"

"A book?" I answered, laughing.

I was nineteen. What was there to write about?

With a warm handshake, we ended our meeting. Again, he repeated, "Trust me, write a book, even if you don't think it's a good idea. You'd be surprised at all the stuff that comes out when you start writing. I know we'll see each other again."

I didn't spend many too many days in Rome, but it was good to lower my stress levels. Some retail therapy was just what the doctor ordered! Believe me; it gave me a lot of pleasure spending the pig's money!

On the way home I thought back to the conversation with Costanzo. I remembered every single word. I remembered his advice. It was refreshing to meet a guy who was interested in my brain and future, instead of what was inside my tight micro dress. "Eva," I said to myself. "One day, you will return here."

CHAPTER 14

WHEN I RETURNED HOME, I decided that it was time to leave this shithole behind. Since it seemed that only people of a 'certain taste' accepted me, I decided to hit the French Riviera and Sardinia; let my hair down and have a good time.

I had just met a smart girl who, coincidently, was a beautiful, blond Venetian, with a penchant for the international and a desire to live out of the ordinary. She was an adventurous business woman, who owned a yacht, on which I had the chance to meet people from all walks of life. This Venus loved to organize parties and participate in multiple events, especially with her friends, who came from the music industry, especially rap music. That period of my life was a great experience, and gave me the boost I needed.

There was a gentle tap on my shoulder, as I was sipping a cappuccino in my favorite bar. When I turned, without having the time to react, I felt a pleasant kiss on my lips. This was Carson, an American sergeant who I had met before and clicked instantly with. Unfortunately we never got it on, because he had to go to Afghanistan. Carson was sure one of a kind. He was the son of some wealthy New Yorkers. He enlisted a month after the attack on the twin towers. I never understood why he just didn't go and work in an office of his daddy's friends, stay outta trouble and have a quiet life. I guess that's American patriotism for you. Your typical American would walk through hell to protect the stars and stripes. So a few weeks later, there he was, kicking the Taliban's ass in the middle of the desert. This made him even more attractive to me. Previously, I had been used to whiny little boys and over-sensitive douche bags, who would throw feisty tantrums if daddy gave them the car without gas; the kind of Grade A prima donnas, who would spend more time in the restroom than my friends.

My prince charming had arrived, on a white horse and an assault gun in his hand! And get this! He also loved me back. Now that he had finished his service he intended to spend some downtime travelling, before going into business or perhaps becoming an officer. He wanted me to follow him in his travels. How could I say no? Carson knew the Big Country real good, showing me all the sights and sounds of places, whose existence, I had never heard of before. I was ecstatic. Carson was a traditional, but generous guy, who turned his nose up the thought of a woman picking up the tab. I think it threatened his manhood but, hey, if it made him happy, it made me happy.

While were hitting off together, his folks saw me as smoke in their eyes. As far as they were concerned, I was just this common Italian, from a fallen family, without a degree. Or prospects. It seemed that, in their eyes, I didn't inspire affection. Whenever Carson called his folks, a soap opera would start up on the other side of the line. It was as if he didn't have the right to date who the hell he wanted. He was twenty-nine! I could see it was a tough balancing act for him. Following those tempestuous phone calls, he'd be moody for hours. Nothing I said, nor those picturesque places we saw, could take his mind off this growing torment. I couldn't see the bright side to the situation. I spent the rest of the holiday brooding, wondering what it was with families, trying to ruin people's lives?

When he went back to America to finish his service, I didn't feel reassured about our status. I was afraid, that because of the age difference of nine years, he would be influenced by his mother and sisters. I was convinced that those prudes would do anything to break us up. So I found myself, the good and faithful girlfriend, on the other end of the phone, listening to him trying to find reasons to break up with me. Why didn't he have the balls to tell me to my face, before setting off for the good ol' US of A? I could tell from his passive-aggressive tone and how he muttered.

"A movie school?! Don't you already have enough qualifications? What the hell do you want, another piece of paper?!" he flared.

"Carson, you don't understand. It's been my dream for a long time. The army could pay for my accommodation at the school. Listen, it's time I did something for me. Why can't you understand this? Do you want to do this or not?"

What an asshole! I couldn't understand his paranoia! Why didn't he get what I was saying? I knew his family were trying to turn him against me. They weren't interested in getting to know me. One minute he was against me coming over, the next he already had my bags packed. I knew this guy. I knew what he was thinking. I tried reasoning with him.

"Carson, you know I love you, but you have to think about our future! You're almost thirty! You're not a kid anymore. You tell me that you want me to come and live with you but, I got news, love doesn't pay the bills! I guess we can live on our savings but it won't carry us forever. Do you know how much it costs to live in the Big Apple? Tell me what you want."

"Why don't you get a job as a waitress, like, at Hooters? With your body it sure won't be a problem!"

With those words, I felt myself dying inside. All the effort I had made to spiritually grow and advance my career, and there was this guy, my guy, suggesting that I display my booty to any ol' bunch of hornies for a lousy tip, like I was a piece of trash. He could not be fucking serious. Did he expect me to come back home every night and warm his soup, after he had spent the day, slumming it with the radical chic crew? No, thanks. For the last time, I tried to appeal to him, asking him if it wasn't better for him, in the short term, staying on with the military, until we had enough dough and time to get used to our new life. I guess he couldn't take it anymore. The war had changed him, as it does to everyone who sees action. It had sapped the energy in his body and mind. We finally managed to see each other a few weeks later. With tears in our eyes, I took his hand.

"I'm sorry, Carson, but I wouldn't ever be able to forgive myself, if I did this to us," I said, getting to my feet and trying to maintain my courage, although my legs were shaking. "I can't stay here. I can't accept your proposal. It isn't going to work out."

I seemed cold, but inside I was falling. I tried to reject this love as too special and important to ruin by rushing into things; getting into something that was way over our heads, but also like a child, that you unconditionally love, but have to kill to save them from more heartache in the future. Carson looked at me half-dazed. I could see the gears of his brain turning, trying to take in the idea that the woman he loved was fearlessly refusing his proposal to live together in New York, in an American dream.

It was his dream, not mine.

"I don't understand," he said finally. His agitation was palpable and heart-breaking. "I can't believe this! Why are you pushing me away now? What do you think you'll find out there? Look around, Eva! It's like, a crazy world out there. You think you'll find something better? You think you'll find a world ready and waiting to receive you with open arms? Fuck, I love you!"

I loved him too. He was the first man with whom I can truly say I really *made love*. Body and soul. It was first time I really experienced some extraordinary orgasms. I remembered one time we were so overwhelmed by our appetite, that we didn't notice the skylight opening above our bed, letting the rain caress our naked passion. Neither of us closed the skylight that evening. We continued, as if our joined physique and technique were being baptised. Despite these wonderful memories that made my soul cry, I had come to the obvious conclusion that, while he was in love with me, he was also, despite the age difference, a little spoiled and immature. I didn't feel that he would be able to hack a serious relationship at this stage or knew what he wanted to do with his career. He wouldn't have been satisfied with me. If I'd have stayed there, at that time, wasting away in some Hooters' bar, I'd have probably wound up like one of those whoremongers, harassing twenty-something chicks and smashing my liver for a home run with crappy, whisky, sourced from, like, the worst 7-11 shop ever.

I walked out of his house and his life, desperately crying. I still remember his famous last words: "When I can give you the life you deserve, I will find you, Eva. I will love you, always."

In my heart, I knew I had made the right choice, otherwise I would have lost that little bit of dignity that still helps me to walk proudly today. It took me years to get over it. Sometimes, I look back on that episode of my life with affection and gratitude. We have to take hits like this, every once in a while, to remind us that we're human, that we have a heart and that we can take these experiences to grow the one, true, lasting relationship we have been searching for all our lives. Call it destiny, call it fate, but I believe that we have to listen to what our soul is telling us as much, if not more, than the heart.

I never knew what happened to Carson. It was better this way, even if a small part of me sometimes wonders how it might have been, had I stayed?

CHAPTER 15

I SPENT THE FOLLOWING MONTHS licking my wounds in Sardinia, where I was constantly being approached by wealthy men, who were pretty interested in my company. I went to the most exclusive and elegant places around the Emerald Coast, like the Millionaire Club and the SottoV, and other fashionable places, where middle aged men, fascinating and above all funny, did everything they could to make me feel admired and pampered, even if they misunderstood why I was there.

I wasn't an escort, I wasn't a philanthropist, I wasn't famous, but I was everywhere. I became known as 'Scarlett', a name given to me by Nicola (Nick) P, the greatest PR at that time (and maybe still) in Italy. Nicola admired me deeply. I became his confidant during that hot Sardinian summer. We'd spend hours chatting. He really loved my massages, especially when I took care of his knee injury. An odd friendship was born; a platonic love (at least that's what I felt for him). I couldn't quite describe what it was exactly that I found so platonically attractive. I learned so much from him, about the ways of the world and the motivations of other people. He was a master of life and helped me understand how to focus, who I wanted to be and how to use my personality to be top dog in the world of public relations. I've always admired people with strong personalities and intellect. We live in an age today where stupidity and ignorance is rewarded and facts are something that are inconvenient. Fight fire with facts, not fire!

So I was still an easy target in those days, because I didn't have a manager or a steady lover who could lead me up some ivory tower. Being a beautiful girl in Sardinia, without allies, without knowledge can be a dangerous game, if you don't know the rules and there's no-one looking out for you. Luckily I knew what I was up against and how to handle myself. There was no way in hell I was going to share the fate of some of the other poor girls with big ideas; getting nailed on the beach by their casual lover (and his friends) for the price of a drink, before settling down to become a flawless, but embittered lady, with a past to hide and a row of skeletons hanging in her closet.

I decided the time had come to go back home for a while. I wasn't enthusiastic about it. The summer was ending and I was getting pissed with the fake 'emerald' life.

CHAPTER 16

T HINGS CHANGED DRASTICALLY, ONCE home. I hooked up with Ryan, a Blackwater contractor. Or to put it simpler: a mercenary! Was this the kind of man strolling around Vicenza these days?!
Ryan was not just a young and handsome man, but a *shark* on the trail of blood: an Adonis cut from marble, which made me melt like ice in the sun. I decided to have some fun with him. Thus the merry-go round of passion began again. After my last love affair with Carson, I kinda struggled to let myself fully go. I was also trying to find another way to make money because I was sure hellbent on preserving my independence.

I was totally engrossed by Ryan's perilous stories. I guess his ass-slapping bravado was just the thing I needed after the emotional roller-coaster ride with Carson. Ryan's work at Blackwater was on the brink of legality. This was before the awful scandal of the 'Nisour Square Massacre' in 2007. I was enthralled and thrilled by his claims of violence and dangerous missions in the Iraqi desert. I was hooked, biting my finger with childish anticipation as he described, in explicit detail, his exploits. Listening to his stories, and picturing the scenes in my head, was like watching an endless action film. I could see it all: blood in the dust. Boots on the ground. Smoke from a gun. The sweat on the chest. A silhouette in the desert haze. Hearing him talk made the blood run through my veins. (What is it about 'bad' guys that make me and most women go nuts?) Perhaps he unlocked my hunter instinct. Ryan knew very well how to capture my attention, knowing that I would ask for more info, more details; anything just to see that wild look in his eyes, that *bloodlust*, which drove me crazy. No act of violence was off limits for me. I trembled with the desire for *more ferocity, more retribution, more blood*. I also wondered what *extras* were inside his leather briefcase he once brought back from Iraq, following another diabolical mission.

For a while, this strong and violent man was my *solace*. I understood and admired him. He told me how he only ended up in the Army to escape imprisonment. In fact, during a bar fight, he misjudged the power of his fist and almost killed another guy. During the war in the Middle East, the notorious American recruiters were looking for fresh meat. They didn't care too much where this 'meat' came from, as long as they were American citizens and loved their country. One recruiter offered Ryan a 'get out of jail' pass, provided he enlisted for at least five years. Who wouldn't have snapped up that offer? Face it. For any young, wayward guy, a life in the Army can offer you focus, self-confidence, free education, a chance to get ripped, regular cash, fucks, insurance and the knowledge that you're serving God and America. Where do I sign up?! It sure beat being in the slammer for a five year bid, getting hooked on nose candy and being some top dog's bitch for leftover showbiz dust on the toilet pan. Once a kid leaves jail with no prospects, they might face life crawling through garbage in some piss-reeked street alley or getting back in 'the game'. They usually wind back up in the slammer because, compared to life on the street, the penitentiary feels like the fricking Hilton!

So Ryan signed up. In those five years, he became expertly efficient at his work as a sniper. Once his voluntary service was over, his dignity prompted him to give up the regular military. He had seen too many things going wrong, that even the patriotic propaganda couldn't hide from the world's eyes. Some of those kids wouldn't be coming home, except inside a body bag, under a stars and stripes shroud. This mission to 'spread democracy', this so-called 'mission accomplished' declared by Bush, was a fiasco. Ryan knew it, the Army knew it. Even the politicians and voters knew it. On reflection, as with Italy, America, has its own special 'Bella Figura'. What kind of twilight does the beautiful, generous, warm glow of the American smile really hide?

Ryan eventually decided to sell himself and his skills to the highest bidder, a little like those escorts in Sardinia. Apart from the memories, Ryan also left me something more important: a renewed practical wisdom. When he disappeared from circulation for another mission in Iraq, I was forced to reinvent myself. Also, I realized that my money was running out.

By a stroke of luck, one day, two of my old friends bumped into me; *Holistic* masseuses with a *special* flavour, I had met when I was hanging around in Sardinia, during the summer. Natasha and Jennifer had decided to move back to the north and were looking for somewhere to crash. Since I was rarely in my crib, I let them rent a couple of rooms. There was more than enough space anyway. The funny thing was that they actually created a massage parlour in my home (which was totally illegal, without permits). It didn't matter to me, because *officially* I knew nothing, and the house was registered to my boyfriend (who was unaware of this agreement). Their first and fondest customers were from the police. It was yet another absurd but enlightening experience: my friends were simple masseuses in famous hotels of the Emerald Coast. There was nothing dirty about it. It was literally, their job. They had a diploma and everything, and yet, when the clients arrived, they always expected *something more*, and seemed quite upset whenever they didn't get this, 'something more'. Among them were obviously politicians, including highly respected regional and municipal councillors of Veneto, lawyers, surgeons and all the typical circus animals, offering good but dubious money to my friends.

CHAPTER 17

A FTER A FEW WEEKS Ryan returned from Iraq, with two new unexpected guests. Something had changed within him. He was on edge, prone to snapping, telling me that I was not the kind of 'wifey material' he expected. He seemed to have lost that carefree attitude that attracted me to him.

At home, maybe to forget, I was enjoying some crazy, out of control parties every night, often against his will. Maybe it was my immaturity that pissed him off but, in the end, this was the last straw for him. One evening he dumped me out of the blue, taking the TV and a suitcase with him. At least he left me the house. I thought I was strong enough to take another blow but it sure felt like a kick in the teeth. I realized that I couldn't have everything from life. I wanted fame, fortune and security, but I guess my fucked up subconscious longed for insecurity, disappointment and danger. In those days I didn't really analyse what it was about threat and jeopardy that attracted me so much. On the surface, I seemed happy and felt independent, but deep down, I guess I was confused and broken. I needed control. I needed certainty. Life was too important to willingly hand it over to imbeciles and stone cold losers. I wanted to freely laugh and love, but inside I was raging and screaming.

CHAPTER 18

VICENZA LIES CLOSE TO an American base. I've always got along well with Americans, mainly because I've always yearned for a more international way of life and maybe because America represents a place of dreams and fantasy. America has always had that 'you can be anything you want' mentality.

Vicenza never offered me much, nothing but bitterness and bad vibes. Don't get me wrong, I will always love Vicenza but I also hate it. Sometimes we have to escape from a place that we hate, to truly love and appreciate it. We have to be destroyed in the city we were made and be rebuilt in another city. So I 'escaped' to America. I mentally escaped from the cold, conservative arms of Italy, into the confident, caring arms of America. The American base gave me a chance to learn more about the people and to practise my American English. At school, while I was pretty good at English, it was generally taught in a dreary way, which didn't so much encourage conversation but *kill conversation*. Even today in Vicenza, whichever school you go to, especially the state schools, especially the reputable, fashionable institutes, education is *crammed and hammered* into our kids, not encouraged and nurtured. Our children go to school in the morning, yearning to be stimulated and reinvigorated, but by the time they go home, and are *forced* to study by their designer parents, they have already been pounded and nailed by education. Therefore, on the rare occasions when an international teacher/speaker arrives, they *breathe life* into the dusty corridors of classrooms. They breathe their international methods and open minds into these closed minds and closed rooms. Even the teachers are relieved when these illustrious visitors arrive from England, America and Australia.

So one evening, I found myself at the Cuore Matto (Crazy Heart) drinking a cocktail, when I noticed this handsome guy staring at me.

"Sorry, you have something important to tell me or are you just dazed?" I teased in Italian.

"Huh, what?" Not another American!

His name was Chris. He was trying to imitate what he considered to be the classic Italian casual look, but without much success. Anyway, since I was bored, I thought it would be a good opportunity to test his character.

"Do you wanna dance?" I asked him.

At the start, Chris was a curiosity for me; someone to pass the time with. Good guys rarely interest me. I usually fall for tough guys with edge, balls, and an intense streak. Like I said, perhaps I had a fucked up subconscious. As a mathematician and engineer, he was so definitely not my cup of tea. His family had Bulgarian roots but had long since moved to the US. Perhaps his loyalty to the family and decades old communist diktats had encouraged him to be competitive and make something of his life. Therefore, he graduated with a degree and even became the chess champion at West Point University, *annihilating* his opponents. Finally, he was working in a country that made him feel welcome. From his sincere words, I understood that he had a certain desire for a serious relationship, even if he wasn't in any rush. This made him seem interesting to my capricious eyes.

After a few weeks, we got together. Yes, as lovers! He regularly stopped by my place, courting me like a gentleman from the past. I was enticed, but I couldn't comprehend why he never took me to see his pad. I understood the reason when I insisted that he show me where he lived.

He had a splendid villa in the Venetian countryside, with views of the hills. Outside I told him that it was beautiful but he was acting all awkward. I discovered the reason when we entered. Apart from a bathroom and a kitchenette, there was just one giant hammock. In. The. Whole. House. It was disturbing, like one of those horror movies where the killer brings his victim to an isolated place, to get rid of them without problems. Usually when an Italian enters a house they say 'Permisso!' followed by an

'Oh, bella!' After saying 'permisso', I said nothing else. Perhaps the place needed a woman's touch.

Good guy Chris was weird. He was simply out of touch in terms of furniture, art or fashion. Actually, to be fair to the guy, it was the first time he'd been living alone as a civilian, not as a soldier. He had left home at the age of sixteen, lived at the military college and then, when he was ready, left for Falluja, where he remained for almost two years. Once he returned, he was transferred to Germany, where he spent his time in some rundown barracks. In short, the words, *home* and *family*, just weren't in his vocabulary. So I decided to take things into my hands. I wasn't prepared to live like Spartan, let alone like a caveman. I made the best of it, and told him that he had to buy some furniture, in order to call the house, a home. Chris really appreciated my suggestions, and seeing that I knew the best shops in the city, I got the best discounts in the sales. The moment when I realized how much he cared about this relationship was one afternoon inside a crockery and ornaments shop. I had asked him to go and buy some drinking glasses, while I looked at the tablecloths. He returned holding two glasses.

"What the hell are you doing?" I laughed. "What are the guests supposed to drink out of? Their shoes!?"

"Guests? There's only you and I. Two glasses are more than enough."

I was stunned. This was a man who didn't know what money was for, who communicated with the simplicity of a child, and as far as he was concerned, didn't need anyone else *but me* in his life. Don't ask me why, but I felt covered by a strong warmth, and all my cynicism ended in oblivion. Perhaps for the first time, I would have sweet normality.

As you would expect, with Italian style and passion and the grandiose American sentimentality, the wedding was a sumptuous, glorious affair, which certainly made me the talk of the town, in a positive way this time. Only the birth of my beautiful, daughter, Sienna, could top that. She was the sweet icing on the cake. From pregnancy to birth, the experience was a frighteningly wonderful thing, and strongly desired. She was the light that cast out all the ghosts of the past. To this day, Sienna contains the strategic, complex, headstrong will of her father, combined with all the sass, energy and fire of her mother.

I used to often wonder what kind of mother I would be, considering I've always been so fiercely independent. Would motherhood soften me and make me overprotective, like some of the others whom I despised? Or would it invigorate me and make me even more determined? I decided not to give weight to these questions. I wanted to enjoy the happiness while it lasted. I couldn't have known then that this happiness wouldn't last.

In the military, things move so quickly that even the soldiers and contractors of the base never know what to expect next. Vicenza was the nerve center for most of the ongoing operations in the Middle East. People came and went all the time. Nothing was certain. Everyone had to be flexible because who knew what was coming tomorrow?

"They're shipping me to Afghanistan. Probably for a year," my husband said one day, with a dark expression. The world collapsed over me. I tried to climb out of the emotional rubble. How could he leave me right now, when everything was going well and we had a pretty daughter to look after?

I wept for days. How would I cope, alone, without the man in my life, in my arms, keeping me safe at night? I had to snap out of it. Face reality. Slap myself in the face and say: 'Look here, Eva! You married a contractor with a ton of assignments, and a job to do, at a time when the American army are up to their heads in shit, around half the globe. What did you expect it would be like? A walk in the park? Wake up, Eva. Shit just got real.'

It was a shock to think that the world was going against my plans.

CHAPTER 19

THIS CERTAINLY DIDN'T MAKE the parting easier, but I consoled myself by saying that a year wasn't such a long time. With a little girl to look after, my life was coming together.

There was another problem. Inside me I was concealing a strong dislike against those that weren't convinced that I was happy and proud of my husband, serving me and his country. They would look at me with pity, as if there was something *abnormal* about me being happy with an American. To arm myself against the nasty implications that I wasn't patriotic enough, I began to study everything I could about American foreign policy and their recent but controversial conflicts. What I learned was far more complicated than had first appeared from my glass house. On one hand, according to some, I wasn't patriotic enough, but on the other, I was an American puppet. I couldn't win. Some people assumed that because I was married to an American, I was somehow a blond propaganda machine for America, when this couldn't have been further from the truth. I take people how I find them. Sure, I supported and stayed loyal to my husband, but no situation is black and white. Every country in the world has its own demons. Wasn't it Jesus who said, 'he who is without sin, cast the first stone'?

Nevertheless, my strength of mind and self-belief made me perfectly capable of standing firm to my principles. That isn't to say that my values weren't tested. I guess underneath, my involuntary sense of pride and suspicion would later be the ruin of our marriage. Sometimes, I thought Chris loved his country more than me, that *America*, was the *other woman* in the relationship.

Every day, I dreamed of my prince charming's return. Meantime, I had to push away any horny chancers longing to take advantage of Chris's absence. Conveniently, they pretended not to notice the ring on my finger. It was hopeless reaching out to the army wives for support. Some of them were sweet and kind. Indeed I had some pretty wild, exciting times with many of them. Made some real good friends. However, there was a section of army wives, these so-called top ranks, whom, I have to say, *bored me to tears* with their whining, especially the way they treated their poor husbands, as if they were sons still at pre-school. Every conversation had that American whine: 'My husband is like um…My husband figures… My husband is like, like, like…ar, ar, ar, ar…' Give me a break, already! It was like listening to a gaggle of junior high school moms, *competing* and comparing; which kid was involved in the most dangerous mission; which kid had the most bullet wounds; which kid was in hospital, getting his legs handed to him in a bag. Oh puh-lease! Drove me nuts. I just wanted my husband back.

If that wasn't bad enough, these so-called virtuous madams, who boasted how they were *saving themselves*, popping diet pills, and counting the days for when their husbands were on leave, certainly allowed themselves some, shall we say, *extra-marital luxuries*. Naturally, these silky episodes never stopped them happily going to church on Sundays or placing their hands on their hearts, whenever they heard the Star Spangled Banner. I found the hypocrisy revolting. As I've said, I've always detested double standards. Here they were, whining on and on about everything, while their husbands were *risking* their lives at front, while in the evening, gladly, *willingly*, opening their easy thighs for any unlucky guy, who took a shine to their plump asses. Some even got pregnant. I was so mad. The barrack walls sure hid many frustrations. They never fully accepted me. In fact they hated me. Not because they believed I was better than them, or because I didn't dance to their drum; it was because I was an overflowing and brazen Italian, who told people, honestly, what I thought of them to their face.

It's such a waste of time, hiding behind masks. Amongst the Italians, where I was popular, and the most well-known in my city, I had the love of my friends. The ones who profoundly hated me were those who had bagged an American guy, thinking that they had won a golden ticket to the *American Dream*, only to wind up in a gloomy base, in the middle of nowhere, with no action and no shopping mall. These two-faced prudes were always trying to give me *friendly advice* about how to be a proper wife, how to not let myself down. Screw that. They hated that I was able to have fun at the clubs and go to the gym every day. I sure didn't want Chris coming back to an *ugly hag*!

Here's the thing; more than a few frustrated husbands would arrive home (having almost gotten killed) waiting to nail the hot bodied babes they'd said goodbye to, a few months or years before, only to be greeted by sad, pale-faced slobs who, night after night, had buried themselves, inside some cheap microwaved dinner; to forget the guilt at getting boned while their husbands were earning a living thousands of miles away. While this seems harsh, I would have more sympathy for someone honest enough to say; "You know what? I was lonely. I couldn't handle the solitude. I just needed someone to hold me. I'm human. Get over it." What I got thrown into my face were these female fortresses of morality, which claimed one thing, but did *the other*.

Day by day, I realized that there was some kind of informal code at the base; the more one let herself down and dressed badly, the more she was likely to become someone's play thing. (These were apparently the most unthinkable, unpatriotic acts, which betrayed their husbands and the army). The barracks housed nothing but rank hypocrisy and pettiness, based on prudish ethics. If anything, some of these All-American well-kept houses were the most corrupt brothels. I learned of a widespread ritual amongst a small but significant section of brides. Having had their fun, they would repent in the nick of time, the moment they learned that their husbands were returning home. They would, therefore, compensate by accusing their former sweeties of rape or sexual assault. Excellent way to guarantee silence around a vice that, in the army, is a crime against honor! With the sacrifice of a couple of expendable recruits, these kind ladies saved their moral virginity for the privilege of doing it all over again, no sooner than their husbands were boarding the airplane for another tour of duty. I knew for sure about two cases, but I heard from others that this was only the tip of the iceberg.

Instead of being a victim, I was having a great time, without any particular effort. Still, I hated being parted from my love. Firm in my convictions, I knew that God would reward me for my loyalty and my strength of soul. Whenever there was a good deal of gossip about me, for gossip grows like weed, I merely shook it off without bothering. I didn't have time to entertain such third-grade pettiness. Let them drown in their pathetic envy.

CHAPTER 20

THE DAY I PICKED Chris up at the airport, I was over-excited with happiness (and also abstinence). My man was back, and now that he wasn't in some crazy hell on earth zone, there would be no more excuses to delay my urge. I didn't even give him time to greet his family and fellow soldiers, before I had already rushed to throw my arms around his neck, and cover him with kisses. His reaction almost cut off the blood supply to my legs. He revealed what he couldn't wait to do to me, to the extent that his comrades immediately offered their apartment as a joke. But something wasn't right. This passion of his seemed to be an act.

In the car, I was asking him thousands of questions, and giving him the lowdown on the gossip he'd missed. He remained distant. Sure, he laughed in all the right places and participated in the conversation, but he couldn't fool me. It was like there was no soul in his behavior. I decided not to worry about it. Who knew what shitstorm he had been through? Instead of letting him get his breath, I was already torturing him with ten thousand words per second. He wasn't just detached: it was like he was in a coma! I was sure that a beautiful vacation and the love of his family would soon reboot him.

At first I was very understanding, but when I saw that the situation was not improving as rapidly as I wanted to, I started getting angry. Instead of telling him that it would all be okay, and there was no rush, my impatience thrust him deeper into his shell. Despite seeing him like that, and being genuinely worried, I wanted to see the man who had promised to give me and Sienna a happy life. I wanted my old Chris back, not this Chris, who was ruining himself by his own hands. I didn't just feel helpless and frustrated that I couldn't get through to him, but betrayed. Here was a guy who should have been here for me. You see, that was my pride talking. It may seem selfish but I was pissed that this stupid war was ruining everything and had taken the real Chris away from me. Maybe the 'real' Chris never returned from Afghanistan, but was still fighting the war. All over the world, soldiers' wives could tell you a similar story. I did nothing but cry. I watched the apathy swallow him up. There was nothing I could do to stop him sinking further into the quick sand. He tried sweetening me up with expensive gifts, based on the assumption that I only needed material things to be happy. I was twenty-three. I was his wife. I was the mother of his child. This forced separation had made me more mature and responsible than him; this stranger. There were still beautiful moments, but he was no longer the Chris of the two glasses. He had become a man that I still loved but who now I could no longer recognize.

CHAPTER 21

ONE AFTERNOON, I WAS taking a stroll with Sienna, when I met him. He appeared from a side street like a mirage, in the sun and sultriness of that lazy afternoon. He was dreamily looking at a newspaper when he noticed that I was, maybe out of boredom, staring at him. Of all the people who were flocking the intersection of Contrà Porti and I had to run into this curious guy!

He gave me such a friendly smile that all I could do was blush. I couldn't even remember the last time a man had smiled at me so sweetly. I was also a little ashamed, since that day, in a hurry, I had left the house wearing a simple outfit. When I saw him turn into Via Porti, I decided to follow him, just to satisfy this strange inviting sense of curiosity. It was stupid! There I was, with the girl in the pram, and I was acting like a teenager with hearts in her eyes. An uncomfortable sense of shame came over me and I turned into a side street. I had to let this go and cool my head down. I was making a fool of myself in front of my daughter. I felt like shit, but deep in my heart, I also felt the compulsion to go back to the time I was a little girl again, wrapped in the safe blanket of Aesop's tales. I was depressed and alone, with my marriage falling apart. And there, in a matter of seconds, my newfound Lancelot had disappeared in a cloud of smoke, and my bust ego vanished in the haze.

As luck would have it, I met this handsome stranger by chance, a few months later, while I was out with friends. I didn't immediately recognize him. I'd had a few shots and wasn't in a good mood. Just as I was looking for someone to save me and light my cigarette, it seemed like this was the evening *everyone* had chosen to be a non-smoker. I was about to put away the cigarette when a hand suddenly stretched out, providing me with the light I desired. It was a nightmare to discover that he was *another* American, even if from his appearance and manner, he looked more like an English Lord. This gentleman simply leaked elegance, with his perfectly tailored dress and relaxed gestures. His name was Timothy. He flirted with me, despite the fact he had previously seen me with my wedding ring and baby.

"Hey, you're really beautiful! I like your dress! Much better than what you were wearing last time."

"Maybe because today I'm not buying milk and looking after my daughter? This is how I look naturally!"

"I'm Timothy!"

"And?"

With a little help from the alcohol and my natural tendency to be a pain in the ass, I felt it was my duty to be a little insolent. I enjoyed this game. Men and women still get jealous today when they see me enjoying attention, but I I know my limits. Anyways, Chris hadn't been paying me much attention lately. It was nice being made to feel that I was still attractive and that I still mattered. There were rare times Chris came looking for me, as if he were doing me a favour, but his erotic play had, by then, grown old. We hadn't slept together for a while. Even when we slept together, I couldn't give him the affection he wanted. It felt like I was doing it out of duty. The passion had ebbed away.

Timothy would have been my secret and happy little island in the boredom that was becoming my existence. Or it would have been a test, to see if still I loved my husband. To him, I think it was more than a challenge, testing whether he could resist jumping on me. It was a mistake to restrain ourselves, because our frequent encounters often turned from a playful friendship into an obsessive wave of lust. I was only held back by the love for my daughter, Sienna. Even so, I couldn't escape the feeling that it was a mistake not to consummate this lust.

In June, Chris and I had already separated. While we still lived under the same roof, Chris didn't want to give up. He asked for one more chance to fix our dying marriage. He decided to take me on a cruise across the Mediterranean, where he spoiled me real good, in a manner which I found a bit embarrassing. It seemed like he was desperate and he was trying to force me to feel something that was already out to sea. Since I wanted to make my marriage work, I made a good effort. I desperately wanted my husband back. I knew, in my heart that he was the man of my life, and that if our relationship improved, we would live happily ever after. However, when I looked into his deep, beautiful eyes, so big and dark, I no longer felt the love between a wife and husband, but a sister and brother. It was wrong to delude ourselves. So, I made one of the hardest decisions I've ever had to make in my life: I left him. I loved him.

CHAPTER 22

"I ALSO THINK THAT SIENNA should stay with you," he said. "I'll probably have to go on another tour of duty soon," he added, with a broken sigh. "What do you want to do about the house and everything else?"

"Don't worry. Everything is yours."

The lawyer who took care of our case was convinced that I was wrong to leave everything to Chris. He took me to one side and said: "Eva, apart from pretty a good alimony check, you won't get anything. Don't be foolish! Take the house!"

"I don't want to live in that house anymore. There are too many ghosts. It's too painful," I said.

It was a big deal leaving that house, which I imagined would have been mine forever. Even as I was laying in Timothy's arms, that thought polluted my mind. For a long time. Home is no longer a home without a heart. This might sound like one of those stupid things you read in a gift card someone gives you, to celebrate your new house, but there's no way this can be denied.

It had only been a few weeks and already someone had been opening their mouths! It certainly wasn't Chris because he was in Afghanistan, probably up to his neck in shit. Now we had another tricky situation to deal with.

Since Sienna and I didn't have another home to go to, we had to stay with Timothy. Chris and I weren't officially divorced yet and Timothy was supposed to keep his distance from me, during the separation which, under the American law, wasn't considered fully valid yet (the military system is so rigid).

I'm afraid it was partly the fault of our bravado.

"Remember when I took you to that officers' ball in Bamberg? Turns out we got busted," said Timothy.

I might have known, because a few days after the ball, my ex-husband wrote me from Afghanistan: his roommates in Germany had been talking shit, telling him that I was being 'disrespectful'. These squealers must have spilt the beans to someone further up the chain.

"They've already put me under investigation," Timothy continued. "My commander said that he doesn't care what your pussy smells like…" This last remark made us smirk. "But if he catches us together again, my career is toast! He got nothing anyway. There's no evidence. It's all good. What can he do?"

I could see that they had him rattled. I knew why. These same 'superiors' had once covered up a *problem* to protect a pupil, who had under oath, lied to an investigation. Not so much a problem, but a fricking landslide, which would have buried them all, had it come out. Many soldiers, civilians, politicians and enemy combatants have learned the hard lesson over the years: don't fuck with the US military.

"Chill! We'll keep our mouths shut. What are they gonna do, throw us in a pit in Guantanamo?" I said. I was mad inside. "Screw 'em! Don't let these thugs get to you. Really, give a guy a uniform and he thinks he's Superman! Trust me, it will be fine. Let people gossip. Face it! They have nothing else in their lives to get their juices flowing."

Timothy's face became a sunrise.

"You know what?" he realized. "You're right. Whatever will be, will be, hey? When this mess ends, and the divorce comes through, we're gonna turn this thing around! Make up for lost time. Come here, babe!'

Timothy took me in his arms and caressed my hair. I felt safe and needed.

"You're a strong woman," he added, planting a delicate kiss on my head. "…and I wanna spend my life with you. I promise that I'll be good father, and husband. Do you understand what you mean to me?"

I never imagined that I would be excited to hear those words again. It wasn't the last time he would repeat them to me.

When I went to Bamberg, however, I received the first surprise. Timothy had been transferred: indefinitely. Even if his superiors didn't have any evidence of our affair, they basically shipped my guy out, until the high command decided what to do. In other words, nothing. They probably thought we would forget about each other. I found myself alone again, hoping that everything would be resolved for the better. It wasn't easy at all. Without speaking a word of German, only 'Mein Name ist Eva', nor knowing anyone, I found myself like some kinda poor idiot, stalking the cold streets of the German city, with no idea of what to do next. One day I went into a restaurant to take shelter myself from the cold, and there, thanks to my perfect knowledge of moronic German, I was busted in few seconds.

"Italian?" The owner of the place asked. "Judging from your complexion, I'd say you were from Trento."

"Close enough. I'm from Veneto. I thought I was the only Italian in this crazy place. I haven't heard anyone speaking Italian for months," I said.

"There are more Italians in Bavaria than in my hometown! If you really have nothing to do, you can always hook up with us. There's always something going down; parties, music, fun," the owner suggested.

It was just the thing I needed. I felt so comfy there, that I decided to treat myself to a little vacation, and get Vicenza out of my hair for a while. Staying with these wonderful people made a change from the regular, sad script with Timothy and previous lovers: up and down dramas, nervous breakdowns, breaking up and making up, the predictable tension following the missions...I would have fled to Italy if it hadn't been for this Bavarian crowd, supporting me. I couldn't return to Vicenza, though. Not yet. It would've been like admitting failure. Everyone, I was sure, would point at me and gossip behind my back. I wouldn't give them the satisfaction.

I was loved by the Italian community in this small gem of a town, but at the same time I was suspiciously viewed by the military. Since that fateful dance in Bamberg that night, the issues many people had about me, gradually turned into a full-scale witch hunt. Although no one would admit it to me in the open, I knew that people were talking about me. These hushed corridor voices had leaked into some indiscreet ears. It was partly my fault, as I was still using the ID Chris had handed to me, to take advantage of basic access, and the kindergarten for little Sienna. Colonel Webb's wife was particularly 'not cool' with my presence in Bamberg. I only discovered this when Timothy called me from Afghanistan.

"Guess who came to see me today, at the front?" He told me, with a rage barely concealed by irony.

"Wait! Don't tell me! Obama finally paid you a visit!" I answered, trying to show some enthusiasm, since it was one of the few times that he shared his opinions with me about life on the front. I knew that many soldiers didn't like this president, as he never got involved with anything unless there were problems. While having always supported the troops, he hadn't put in appearance to see how it was going.

"If only! Nah, we only got His Majesty, the Great Colonel Webb, in flesh and blood!" he spat between his teeth. "Yup, hitched a lift in his armed chopper for an official visit to the camp. Sure didn't come to shoot pool with the guys, have a few Buds and share some locker room talk! The guy was on the war path. Turns out he wanted to see me. What the hell have you been doing, while I was away?"

"Absolutely nothing, I don't understand ..." I started, but then it hit me. "I remember now! At the ball, right... I think his wife was onto you. She was up my ass half the night with questions and questions, like I was some kinda spy! I didn't tell her anything, but hey, who knows what goes on in that air-head of hers!"

"Well thanks to that, I'm now a special guard. And that's not the only good news! We have to relocate soon. We got our orders from the top. Since we're being frisked couldn't you, like, try and stay outta trouble for five minutes, Eva? I mean, is that possible, huh?"

I tried to argue my case, but there was no point. I didn't have any idea what Timothy was really going through out there, but I could guess. Confidentiality is, for the select few, a privilege. Any perceived threat to any mission has to be silenced, neutralised and locked away. It can start with mystery reassignments, some 'friendly advice', and maybe a temporary loss of privileges, like phone calls and passes, but it can also cut deeper if the problem is persistent. In short, if you try and push against the might of the US Army, the US Army will push back. *Harder.* Feeling resigned, I hoped that this would be the last trial which the Lord, in His infinite goodness, wanted me to endure. It was time to get busy. I couldn't go on like this. With the help of that holy man, aka my beloved ex-husband, Chris, I finally got the documents to formalize the divorce from the Texas court. At last! I could breathe a sigh of relief, and with Timothy's eventual return, I was certain that everything was gonna be great again.

The day of our heroes return is a day of joy, in which the partners stay at home with their beautiful family to groom themselves and get ready to see their loved ones. Not only would I refuse to be outdone by the other wives, but as a chic Italian, I would be The Best. With a super elegant tailleur by Dolce & Gabbana, very long platinum hair and my devoted *tacchi dodici* heels, I *owned* every wife.

I preferred leaving Sienna with a friend during the welcoming ceremony, because, after so much suffering, this finally had to be the moment of triumph for me and Timothy. I had my divorce settlement in hand. It was sure to be pleasant surprise for him.

I finally arrived at the sports hall where the ceremony was due to be held. These ceremonies are organized in a very particular way. Separated by a giant white curtain, the wives and husbands wait, as the notes of the American national anthem swell out. From the outside, it may look corny and camp, but when you are there, and you look at the hundreds of military boots, starting to appear under the tarp, the emotion is magnificent. For once, it unites everybody in the base. Suddenly, a woman barged past me, elbowing me out of her way, as she dragged her two, screaming children. Okay, not all of them apparently made an effort to shine; this one for example, in curlers and robe, must have just fallen out of bed. In its own way, instead of pathetic, it was kinda tender. It was easy to recognize Timothy, once the tarPhilliein had been raised. In the midst of so many soldiers, during the crescendo of the hymn, he noticed me from out of the corner of the eye and smiled. By the time the prayer for the fallen ended, I lost sight of him.

As soon as the ceremony officially ended, and the order was given to break the lines, all this solemn composure went to hell. I watched as loved ones threw themselves, almost literally, at the person they had been parted from, never knowing if they would see them again. I also rushed to where I thought Timothy was, but in the midst of such confusion, I lost sight of him. I looked around, searched the eyes, embraces and tears of the reunited. Where was Timothy? Thankfully, he hadn't lost sight of me. I felt his strong arms embracing me from behind.

"I love you," his voice whispered into my ear. "You have no idea how much I missed you! Let's get outta here! I can't take it anymore!"

I dragged him away before he was seized by his fellow comrades. Since he was the company commander, all his non-commissioned officers had to ask him permission to breathe. No sooner than putting his feet on the ground, he would usually be overwhelmed with all kinds of requests. He wanted to stay with me. To avoid being identified by the begging horde, he immediately removed his jacket and cap. We escaped to the comfort of our home, where we made love all day.

As with Chris, the first two weeks were heavenly, like a second honeymoon. When we weren't making love, we were cuddling and spoiling each other. The newfound happiness and the physical relief made everything easier, not to mention the fact that Timothy was always helping me take care of little Sienna. There's a lot I could say about Timothy's misgivings, but I'll tell you one thing: he was an *excellent* stepfather. The problem always comes later, when the fury of passion begins to fade. You have to remember and understand that you're dealing with a person who has spent months in a hellish place, with only the company of his comrades and hostile locals. When a soldier is suddenly catapulted back into harsh reality, it takes time to adapt. For a while everything's too quiet and still. They walk around feeling that they're in a strange limbo. Many hit the bars to get wasted on shots. Many try their luck with local girls. Many get into fights. They want that rush of adrenalin, even when they know it's the last thing they need. As if there weren't already enough misunderstandings between us, Timothy starting giving me the whole 'I need my space' speech, which made me go batshit. In my mind I couldn't understand what was up. Hadn't he already got enough space? How much space did he need anyway? I was like, 'okay, so what does this mean for us?' It turned out that he was also suffering from post-traumatic stress disorder. It was something he couldn't directly admit because it would have cost him his command position. So he kept it all locked away, occasionally venting his anger in the house. The man who had written me fifteen hundred love letters in one year, had turned into a lion in a cage. It was clear that he was no longer in control of his own choices. He was looking for a way out. I had become a burden to him. After lovingly kidnapping me, forcing me to surrender my house and following him on his journey, he could not accept that I was stubborn enough, and not supinely loyal to his whims.

Petty things, like returning home and discovering that the furniture wasn't exactly where he had placed it, had become hard to bear for him. We didn't need many excuses to argue. I could see that he was sincere about trying to resolve our quarrels, out of honor and love, but every day this man I loved was coming undone. He was now a person on the edge of bipolarity. Some days he just needed to fight at all costs. Whatever the bullshit, it was reason enough to attack me. Other times, he was brittle and fragile as a child, begging me, almost on his knees, to never leave him. I was on the edge of a breakdown myself, even physical. I was thin and unmotivated, but I was determined to keep smiling, in front of my daughter. I owed it to Sienna and her father, to hold it together. Wearing a mask, I played the part of the fulfilled woman, hoping, if nothing else, that my goodwill would make the situation bearable.

The only person I told the truth to at the base was the counsellor chaplain, Tyree. At the beginning it was difficult to open up to him. Little by little, I realized that he was nothing more than a good person, who cared about the well-being of others. He also had a soft spot for me. In particular, he was worried about Timothy's behavior, similar to many, many soldiers he had seen before. According to Tyree, Timothy was trying to manipulate me by creating a space around me, in order to control and, consequently, use me as shield against the pressure that oppressed him. A *human shield*, I supposed. It was common and, sadly, a normal thing, Tyree said, that happened to many soldiers who returned from their tour of duty. I had to realize this, to try to understand if it was still possible to do something, or if it was already too late. There was a lot to take in and make sense out of. From my conversations with Tyree, I understood that it was time to go out into the world again, as I wasn't only losing Timothy but myself.

Out here, I had some luck. Many of the friends I had made in Bamberg were sincere and warm hearted people. They understood that I hadn't isolated myself from them on purpose. They knew what it was like, as they too had experienced a few crazy things in their pasts. Like Vicenza, Bamberg was a small city that lived on the back of the army life. We all had similar stories to share. Without these bases scattered all over the world, for our protection, we wouldn't have met our loved ones, but on the other hand, the absolute *terror* of war and conflicts too often has a horrifying effect on our loved ones.

Just when I was convinced by Tyree's words, Timothy caught me off guard.

"Do you remember that trip to the Caribbean I dreamed about, while I was in Afghanistan?" he asked me one day. Before I could answer, he put a pair of air tickets under my nose, to the largest landing strip in Florida, Fort Lauderdale; for the Caribbean. Two tickets for the Princess Ruby, a ship with expensive taste, not one of those dreary Spring Break tubs, full of bourgeois university students and high school dropouts, looking to get their first disappointing lay. How could I say no? Sienna was delighted to have a vacation with her dad and grandparents. It upset me to part from her, even if it wasn't for long, but this vacation was the last chance I had to mend and meld with Timothy, and I wanted to be close to him. It was a grave mistake…

CHAPTER 23

S HORTLY AFTER BOARDING THE ship, I had my first surprise. A distinguished couple approached us on one of the decks. I thought they were just a bored pair who wanted a bit of chit chat, while waiting for the activities in the afternoon, but I immediately realized that they were very close to Timothy, judging from the bear hugs they exchanged.

It turned out that this 'distinguished couple' were his father and his new girlfriend!

"Oh, Eva… I kinda forgot to tell you… Daddy wanted to join us on the cruise! Must have slipped my mind, right?"

Yeah sure, I thought. I recognized the father from an old photo Timothy had shown me a while ago. But why worry? His father was there with his new squeeze, a beautiful and self-confident woman. I figured that he had *other things* to handle than his kid. I was wrong. To say they had taken a shine to us was an understatement. They couldn't leave us alone for a moment! Wherever we went, Daddy and his girl would show up; at the pool; at dinner; during outings. You know, I was even afraid of waking up sometimes and finding them in our bed, between me and Timothy! The famous romantic bungalow, which Timothy had told me about in the letters effectively, existed; on this ship! He had this gig booked for a long time. One time his dad was waiting for us in our cabin, with a plate of jumbo shellfish! It was a nightmare.

Yet again, the worn script of this love story began to repeat itself, going from breaking up to making up sex. When the cruise ended, the ordeal was only just beginning. Since we still had one week of vacation left, Timothy's father suggested we hit San Francisco, where they lived. I accepted, partly to see a city I had heard so much about, partly because I was hoping to carve out some space for myself in this open metropolis and to free myself of these chains. Our famous vacation was just an excuse to see the whole family again, rather than spending quality time repairing our bruised love life. Even in San Francisco I was forced, most of the time, to stay with his folks, including Timothy's peculiar mother. His mom was a former nurse who seemed to have a taste for mixing gin and medicine. She was perhaps the most human of the family, but as much as I liked her, she wasn't easy to bear. I wondered how a woman like her had fallen so deep in shit? She spontaneously gave me the answer one night, after I had got up to take a glass of water. I found her sunken into the armchair in the living room, with a full glass in one hand, and a half-empty bottle in the other. She seemed to be staring into space, as if the whole universe was spinning in her head.

"Can't you sleep, dear?" she slurred, with a smirk.

"Sorry for disturbing you, ma'am. I'm thirsty. I just wanted to see if there was some water or juice in the fridge," I said, hoping that she wouldn't offer brandy. "Are you okay?"

She just shrugged and took another hit from her liquid companion. Her relatives had described her as a weak person, but to me she wasn't at all weak, just sad and hurt.

"You have no idea how much I love my children," she said. "Especially Timothy. I know a mom shouldn't have favourites but it ain't easy. I just hope you don't become an asshole like his father."

I was about to say something, but she lifted her finger.

"Listen, don't be fooled by the pretty face of my ex. He looks like the most regular guy in the world, but in truth, that sonofabitch would slay all of us for thirty pieces of silver. You have no idea what I had to suffer. As if the betrayals weren't enough... all the insults and cheating. Now they treat me like the family fool." She let herself sink into the pillows. "You know? You look a lot like me when I was your age. See that you don't look like me now, in twenty years..."

It wasn't pleasant getting dragged into someone else's soap opera, especially when the holiday had already been like Hades. The relatives, with their fake smiles, did nothing to deny what the lady had told me. Timothy's dad was often hassling his wife, accusing her of having squandered the family fortune (Mom and Dad were from good family, even if they decided to do 'modest' jobs, she as a nurse, and he as a fireman). He didn't miss a chance, usually in front of the children and me, to remind us of the beautiful house they had given up for the bad habits and sins of the lady. It was just too ludicrous to be true. It was clear she had some plastic surgery, but in my opinion, she didn't need it. As a young woman, she was so beautiful and elegant. While it's hard to imagine what she may have looked like without the plastic surgery, I'm sure she would have aged naturally and gracefully. Plastic surgery is rarely, *completely* successful. While I've known some people who have had some amazing cosmetic work done, I've also known some who were very disappointed. As long as you respect the body, the natural ageing process can be beautiful. Sometimes, removing the lines and bags with a scalpel, often removes the *character* and *soul* of a person.

Returning back to Timothy's father... instead of hassling his wife, maybe he could have managed his wife's expenses. Even if he had reason to be pissed at her, what sense was there in continual rebukes and accusations? The children took the side of their father. It was like watching one of those nature programs, where the family turn on the weak.

"You know, maybe it would be better if, like, Mom wasn't a burden on everyone!" Timothy snapped, after yet another speech on the status of family.

"I got ya," his brother replied. "Her life is like shit."

And then, whenever the mother arrived with tea and biscuits, these daggers turned to smiles.

Holy Fucking Cow! I thought: You all wanted her to die, and now ya'll kisses and hugs?! It seems to be the typical, suburban mentality in the US, especially amongst the snobbish smartasses in Alta California. Never show the dirt in public, just play the Happy Family all along, and hope that the devil will take your relatives as soon as possible. The funny thing is, they've convinced themselves that cuckolds and moral corruptions don't actually exist in these neighborhoods. They are all angels. They can do no wrong. But if they feel wronged, the gates of hell are sure opened on those 'evil-doers'.

Maybe, in a sense, Italy is better for this: if someone is an adulterer, for example, people behave accordingly without the Greek tragedy of pretending to be more moral. I guess they keep quiet. Mind you, Vicenza, is not like the rest of Italy. In fact the city is also known as the *anteroom to the Vatican*. It sees itself as super moral and super divine. In many respects, in terms of complexity, America and Vicenza are like twins.

Last stop was Las Vegas, to take the little beloved brother to work: if you called giving flyers to shitfaced tourists, outside drab nightclubs, while pompously calling it public relations, a job in America. Sure beats me. Anyways, I heard so much about Las Vegas. I couldn't miss the opportunity to see it with my own eyes. Lil' brother Mark, besides being a penniless slob, had decided to 'date' (out of all the hot chicks you can find by the dozen in California) a Mexican girl without a residence permit. You can imagine how his super republican father took this. Not a day went by, without that dazzling smile, where he told his boy that Mexican women were pretty much only good for blowing you. Mark didn't get the message, as when we arrived in the city, we discovered that the girl was pregnant with his child. Timothy wasted no time in congratulating and weeping his bro love towards Mark. With a slap on the back, super hugs and touch on the balls, it looked like one of those bad college comedies. I didn't find the scene at all moving.

I took Timothy aside, taking advantage of Mark being in the bathroom, and told him what I thought. I didn't want to get too involved. Timothy's smile turned into an upset mask.

"I sure hope your brother knows what he is doing," I started. "Just wait 'til he sees how difficult it is to raise child and how much it costs. Anyone with a brain would leave that dump where he lives."

Timothy replied, "Then he will take his responsibilities. I'll help him get straight. I got his back."

"Timothy, you know that responsibilities are taken *before* having a child, not after, right? You going to babysit him, for the rest of his life? Where do you think you'll find the money? From our savings?" I said, not liking what he was suggesting.

"Don't fucking talk about my bro like that!" he snarled. "It's his life, right? His fucking business!"

"No, darling, it's *our* business, if we start handing out our money. Besides, isn't your brother's girl also a friend of yours?" I asked provocatively.

"Huh? We heard about her, that's all. I guess we didn't think it would lead to anything like this," said Timothy.

"You're fake! You should have been more honest with him! Now he's gotten himself into something that will probably stay with him for the rest of his life!" I said. 'I'll bet they don't even love each other."

Timothy seemed to understand that I was right, but he continued to defend his brother. It's really true that hope is the last thing to die. He was still convinced that he could, from one day to the next, put his head in the right place, find a real job and become a perfect guy. All of a sudden Mark arrived, interrupting our conversation. I just couldn't keep my thoughts lingering. Since it was impossible for me to rub Mark's nose in bullshit, I spoke to him like a mother to a friend.

I turned to lil' brother during dinner. "Great news, hey? It's fantastic. So! Where are you planning to live?"

Mark looked at me, as if his Mexican babe had just crawled out of my nose. I proceeded to explain what I meant.

"Las Vegas isn't the sweet life, if you can't handle yourself. You'll need to find a secure day job that pays well. You can't leave your wife and whining baby, while you go around all night, giving flyers to runaways hoping for somewhere to party, after getting hitched by some fat wino in a snug Elvis Presley costume."

His face turned white as a sheet. He clearly hadn't even taken the most basic necessities into consideration. At my side, however, Timothy had taken on all the color his brother had lost, when he realized I had side-stepped his caution. I didn't get to finish what I was saying. Timothy's eyes turned me into stone. I was only trying to be well-meaning. Use some humour. Apparently, such advice is not appreciated these days. I was only trying to put things in perspective, since I was experienced in these matters. I guess the words of a streetwise and sexy Italian girl, wasn't worth shit in a place like this.

"Well, anyway, cheers! Here's to Mark's new life!" I toasted, with a forced smile.

From their faces, they clearly hadn't understood my good intentions. Mark almost fainted on the table. It was times like this I wondered what the hell I was doing here, wading into family problems when we had problems of our own. After this little dinner drama resumed, we toasted our future ventures in Sin City.

Vegas truly comes to life at night. With its depth of color, lights and sounds, even the most luscious movie doesn't come close. It's absolutely unreal; a gigantic comic that forever seems to grow in size. It's like a galactic kaleidoscope of humanity, so vulgar and yet so fascinating. Everywhere you go, it's all there; casinos, alcohol, luxury cars, gondolas in the middle of the desert and pyramids that seem to reach out from nowhere. Every hotel is like a gigantic shopping mall, and the best are connected to each other like a beehive, making it possible to literally walk miles without going outside. It's beautiful and terrifying. Las Vegas is also hell on earth. Once your eyes get used to the bright lights, you start to distinguish life in the creeping shadows from the fake glow of the glitz and glamour. It's more like Lunar Park than a bustling metropolis. I honestly didn't know how Timothy's brother was able to survive without being chewed up and spat out by this sleazy, ruthless monster. It was enough to see the waitresses, often middle-aged, moving catatonically between the tables, as if they'd mentally given up decades ago. As you watched the escorts float like spectres, it was clear that they too had made some kinda life, and that for every one who'd made it, a thousand more had fallen and become slaves of their failure; doomed to serve drinks to slot machine junkies, even more desperate than them, while they flushed months of earnings down the 'john' to chase that lucky jackpot.

At the entrance of the disco, where Mark worked, was the manager, checking the VIP list. He gave us a dazzling smile. "Mark, who's this little creature with you? She doesn't look like your typical ticket."

"This is Eva, my future sister-in-law. She's from Italy," answered Mark, breasting up, happy to be able to strut a little in front of his colleagues. "She's staying with my brother, you know?"

I was stunned. After these pleasantries, we were shoved into the *normal* row, instead of the VIP one, Mark had promised us. To hell with all that baloney! According to him, with all money he made at the club, he could really afford Vegas. Timothy, meanwhile, wore a worried expression. The whole image of a brother being able to comfortably get by was slowly shattering before his eyes. I tried to relax, as much as was possible. At one point, I saw the manager nodding at me. Since Timothy was busy, talking to his friends, I went over to see what he was gawking at.

"What the hell are you doing in the middle of those losers? You should be here in the VIP row, among the beautiful girls!"

"True, but I guess since Mark works here, I thought we would be able to go right in," I said.

The manager took on an expression of pity.

"Mark? Not...oh yeah, the guy you were with! Yup, I understand... but look...he only delivers flyers for the restaurant. He has nothing to do with the big stuff!"

All my worst fears had been confirmed in a few seconds. Mark, who spoke like a great man, who prided himself being best buddies with the manager, barely knew him. I thanked the manager for the chat, and proudly took advantage of his offer to skip the line.

We walked past tables, taking advantage of Mark's familiarity of the place. Timothy paid for everything. Alcohol gushed in rivers, and thanks to a few discounts, we probably had one shot too many. Especially me, since I didn't have much experience drinking myself under the table. Timothy and Mark were really hitting the hooch, like a couple of Irish studs. I couldn't understand how they were still standing.

I went to the bathroom to freshen up. I was tired, and needed a bit of timeout from the crowd. My cell phone showed that it was four in the morning. Maybe it was better to go home, considering how wasted the other two were. Besides, I was looking forward to hitting the pool later. Topping up the tan.

It took me a while to find Timothy but Mark was nowhere to be seen. One thing at a time, I thought. Timothy didn't look too good. Crashed out on a sofa, he totally looked like shit. I hoped I wouldn't have to carry him to a cab. I shook him gently. It took him a while to recognise me. Eventually, he straightened up and rubbed his eyes. He seemed able to walk without help.

"Timothy, it's time to go. I'm exhausted. It's super late. Let's go find Mark and go home," I said.

"He's long gone, girl! You made him run away with your paranoia!" he blurted, out of the blue. "You're just jealous!"

I tried to stay calm. He was drunk. I didn't want to pass the last night arguing.

"Hey, come on, babe! There's no need for bad vibes. Let's wait a while, see if Mark turns up. If not you can go check the restroom."

His tone of voice stung me. *In vino veritas*, we say in Italian, which is essentially 'booze talking' or 'alcohol reveals the truth.' I doubt he would have ever had the courage to talk to me like that when he was sober.

"Yeah, yeah, whatever! Get off my case, huh? Why you have to go and talk shit like that? Christ, the guy is just getting used to being a daddy! Would it kill you to be happy for the guy? Jeez, I can't understand you, sometimes!"

I tried reasoning with him and calming him down, but it was impossible now he was on a roll. He began mumbling more nonsense, becoming more and more agitated. I couldn't figure out what the hell he was talking about.

In the end, he shouted at me very clearly: "This is your fucking fault, bitch! Now find my fucking brother right away, or I swear to God, I'll fucking leave you… in this dump, and you can fucking hustle your way back to some motel! Hey, what's up? Don't you fucking understand good ol' American? Huh? Wanna cry, huh? You wanna go get the mafia on my ass? Why are you fucking standing there? Go get my brother back!"

There and then, months and months of repressed anger exploded all at once. In one blow. All the frustrations, insults, humiliations and the lies I had endured, melted into a blind rage. For the first time in my life, my body reacted almost by itself. I punched that cunt right in the face. The scene was more comical than anything else. There I was, small and half-drunk, trying to smash this muscle mountain in front of me. The blow had surely taken him by surprise, so much so, that he took a step back, tripped and fell on the sofa. At that moment, I felt relieved. A few seconds later, I realized that it was not the relief of the punch, but the hands of a hulking bouncer, who literally lifted me, but not quite as literally, threw me out of the club!

After the adrenaline wore off, shame wore me like a jacket. There wasn't a person in that colossal corridor, who wasn't staring at me. I tried to recover, but slipped. I quickly got to my feet and, in a moment of dignity, quickly checked my nails, swept my hair, and retreated in style. Staying there, in the blinding lights of the corridor, with the distorted faces of the people around me and all the confusing thoughts going around my head, was a waste of time. I couldn't be bothered trying to return to collect Timothy. Not after that scene.

The adrenaline fell, leaving me exhausted. I found a place to catch my breath on the edge of a splendid fountain. Slowly my mind cleared, helped by the placid sound of the water. I realized that I had reached a point of no return. How was I supposed to get out of this mess? In a foreign country, surrounded by mean people and with a life gone south, I felt overwhelmed. It took me a while to realize that Timothy was actually sitting next to me. His anger must have subsided because at that moment he was dejected. The tension was still solid. We were too tired for a moment of truce. We remained immersed in that awkward silence, before he took the initiative.

"Come on, let's go to sleep," he said.

In that moment, this seemed to be the most sensible option in the world.

Returning to the hotel, still shaken by nerves and too drained to react, I wondered if, in that city, there existed someone even more miserable than me. I soon got the answer once I reached the lobby. At the machines that lined the walls, a middle-aged gray man was still sitting in the same place we had seen him eight hours previously, when we left the hotel for the evening. Now it was almost dawn. Quite mechanically, the little man inserted a coin into the slot, pulled the lever, and threw a little curse when the blindfolded goddess decided that it still wasn't his lucky day. It seemed that the machines were sucking his life as much as his wallet.

Timothy and I didn't have much time to talk about the incident, the night before. We had to pack and take the flight home. I couldn't wait to hug my daughter. Her unconditional affection, I was sure, would banish this nightmarish vacation. I was even ashamed to look at Timothy because of the slight bruise on the cheek, where I had struck him. This made me feel embarrassed and morose on the flight back home.

Once I crashed on the bed, I was finally relieved to fall into a deep sleep with my treasured daughter in my arms.

CHAPTER 24

W HEN HE TOLD ME that he was being transferred to another remote hole, I stupidly imagined that it would have been like moving from Vicenza to Verona, or some other fairly secluded village. Instead, we wound up in the darkest part of Bavaria; Grafenwoehr; a town so small that it only had one supermarket and a church. On the other hand, since it was a military place, it didn't lack discos and lap dancers! It took me a month not to misspell its name.

At the beginning of October, we were welcomed by a heavy snowfall. I had never been to Eastern Europe before, but this place *seemed* to be straight out of the worst anti-Soviet propaganda films. We were precisely in the golden triangle of European manufacturing. It couldn't be said that this place was badly kept, or particularly sordid, but it was one of the saddest villages I've ever seen in my life. The average Venetian village is certainly not known for its vitality, but between fairs, village festivals and some herds of wild cyclists, there's usally a funny hue to the place. Here however, there was absolutely no soul. It was like the land of the dead. A pallid gray hung over everything. Everything you would usually associate with pre-1989 Eastern Europe could be applied to this place: old, abandoned rusting cars by the roadside; narrow empty streets with torn posters; advertising long forgotten events, flickering in the wind; depressed looking old women carrying stale bread; suspicious glances and whispers on the corner; unsmiling children, wearing the handmade fashions of their grandparents; crumbling paintwork on the walls and houses; life in catatonic motion.

From the car, I had already noticed how isolated it was, given the time it took us to reach the town, but that wasn't a big problem. Actually, at the beginning, I saw it as a good opportunity; however this place wasn't my style, considering how social I was. I tried to see it as a quirky vacation. Maybe I could use the time to think seriously about everything that I was going through, without the anguish of having to live under investigation, given the much coveted divorce. I realized how wrong I was, as soon as I stepped out of the car. Within seconds, we had everyone's eyes on us. We were the ones who had gotten away with it! Our secrets were branded on our faces! We were Strangers. Outsiders. The Uninvited. It was in that low budget horror film atmosphere, that we began this new period of our life.

There is nothing more relaxing, in this world, than a nice hot bath, to take your mind off the stress. You just have to let the hot water rock you; rock those thoughts away. Let your body slide under the surface, inch by inch, little by little, and enjoy the strange feeling, as if you were back in the womb. Let all the negative thoughts disappear. For a little while, you can forget where you are, who you are and how you got there. In the world of water and relaxation, time seems to stop. You exist in a dreamlike state, like that moment just before you open your eyes in the morning and become fully conscious. You enter into a deep world, a deep state, immersed in tranquillity and at unity with everything. For a few moments, nothing matters. For barely a second, the universe flows through you and all things exist in a breath. Pain disappears, pleasure dissolves but no-one suffers. All guilt, regrets, and heartaches simply vanish under the bubbles and, for a split second, everything is unfiltered.

Many women would have been happy having my opportunities; young, beautiful, and with a fairly high standard of living. So why wasn't I happy? What more could I want?

It was so cold. Even when the fireplace was raging and the stove had been switched on, I could feel the icy caress of the winter mistress on my skin. Meanwhile, I tried to keep myself motivated, getting in shape, looking after my daughter, fixing my makeup and spending as much time as possible on every detail; staying active, without leaving anything out. I had every reason to pull myself together. It isn't within my vocabulary to give up. Keeping a scrupulous routine helps me a lot: it was the only way not sit in an armchair and sink inside it, until I became part of the furniture myself. I thought about Timothy's mom and how I didn't want that to happen to me. I had to stay busy. This place and the dank sky sure weren't good for my nerves. I felt like I was being challenged, to hold it together. How deluded I was! I thought of the old lovers I had left, because I couldn't face a miserable future. And yet, here I was. I had completely fallen into the same trap from which I had been fleeing all my life! The tentacles were reaching out for me again.

CHAPTER 25

EVERY DAY WAS OCCUPIED with Sienna. Mother and daughter. Together. It felt good. It made a change from crazy nights out or bitching with America's Next Miss Patriot. I strolled around the base, chatting to people about everything. Normal everyday things, you know? With everyday people.

In this small village, I was surprised to find quite a number of citizens of mixed race, derived, I presumed, from the spellbound passion of the German women for the beautiful African-American pilots. Italy, like Eastern Europe, isn't as multicultural as you imagine. It's certainly nowhere near as diversely rich as America, England, Germany or France. The Italians are a suspicious people, especially of (gli altri) *other Italians*, never mind those from other continents. This wary, provincial nature is everywhere you go, from next door neighbours to the nearest region. When it comes to those with a darker complexion, this Italian guardedness often transforms into hostility. Italy, by accident or by design, is one of the most prejudiced countries in Europe. Open up the papers, watch the television, walk down the street, listen to the people and politicians, and you'll see multi-cultures being buried, wiped away, forgotten about, hated, denied access, abused, laughed at, shot at, you name it. You'd be lucky to find someone of African origin employed even in the most basic roles, let alone in a high-powered position of responsibility. The eyes of Italy often look to other western countries for constant approval and praise, without looking inwardly. My country hasn't fully come to terms with The Second World War.

In the playground, I would often chat amiably with young mothers.

I got to know most of them well, especially one group of single mothers of a Pacific and West Indian origin. I was surprised to discover that these girls had nothing to do with the US base. For generations, ever since the Second World War, many underprivileged German women would fall in love with Americans stationed at the base. Often, the Americans would weave the girls some tall tales about life in the big city, before disappearing; leaving the new mothers to fend for themselves, having used their warm and welcoming German flesh to keep them warm, during the brutal winter months. There were of course some lucky girls who found their dream ticket and escaped to the Land of the Free with Prince Charming. From what I was told this practice still hadn't declined. Wherever you go, in any US Air base, you will find some women looking for love and escape, but pressured into dubious occupations to make ends meet; Barrack bunnies, Jo whores; each base has their own terms to define these unfortunate girls. However, no-one has come up with the term to define how to solve this problem, since nobody could care less. Perhaps the lucky ones return home and are forgiven by the family, while others look towards God and His Mercy to find the answers.

Little by little, my indifference changed in a mixture of sadness and panic. Even though I believed that I was secure and privileged, I seriously began to fear that I was doomed to share the same fate of so many poor girls before me. Continuous quarrels, Timothy's lies and uncertainties about the future, made me feel our story was ending and it wouldn't be nice and smooth. The straw that broke the camel's back was when I met the beautiful Caroline. She was an exotic beauty, an eclectic mix of Caucasian and Africans traits. At twenty-one years of age, she had many dreams and hopes but still lived with her mother, who helped her and her little girl. She was quite the expert at nail manicures and fixing hair extensions. Despite this, she could aim higher in my opinion. I met her when she came to do my nails at home. She was easy to talk to because she was educated; she spoke three languages and knew something about everything, which alleviated my terrible boredom. Once she felt able to trust me, she told me that her child was also a daughter from the base. I understood the trap she had fallen into. For a girl like Caroline, it was even more difficult to climb out of the chasm. I was also worried when she told me that she had fallen in love with some private at the air base, some loser with big ideas.

I have nothing against privates but until they're promoted, they usually don't have enough money to hold a family together. So it wasn't my place to intrude. On the contrary, I hoped that this guy was the right person for her. I was sorry to see a beautiful person like her suffering.

By some strange coincidence, I once passed her and her boyfriend on my way to the club. They were arguing outside the entrance, because, as I understood it, she had caught him flirting with another girl.

"How can you do me this, after getting me pregnant!" she screamed.

With a sneer, the private replied, "I'm not gonna do this right now. We'll talk about it tomorrow."

He staggered towards the entrance of the base, the famous impenetrable limit for the underprivileged. It wasn't just a strategic retreat for the private but more of a slink, with his tail between his legs. Caroline caught my eye and threw her arms around me. She sure had it bad for him.

"Hey, don't worry," I said, hugging her tightly. "If you want to look for him, I can get you in the base, okay? But you have to stay calm. Don't throw a tantrum or you risk sending everything upstream"

I continued to console her, but at the same time, I couldn't forget about the child. I never knew how it ended, because I never saw Caroline again. This story was like a cold shower, and made me understand that nothing could be taken for granted. It gave me the shock I needed. I had no intention of winding up like Caroline. I understood that no matter how educated and well-mannered she seemed, she was still just another 'dormitory bunny', disguised as an official wife, which I certainly was not.

Timothy was already asleep when I got home. I booted up the computer and looked at the photos of our happy times. Perhaps I was trying to get that worm off my back, that demon who was trying to burrow into my soul. I put on a nice romantic piece of music called *Angel of the Moon*, which was our song. It always gave me a pleasant thrill, but that evening it couldn't give me the comfort I needed. It was there, in the glare of the screen, with the reflections and images of happier times, dancing over my face, that I felt inspired. Or perhaps it was paranoia. In any case, it was better to prepare for the worst. I took a USB stick from the drawer, and started to download all the photos, videos and documents of the joint rentals and current accounts we had opened together. I can't say why exactly, but I felt a sense of peace that I hadn't felt for months, a sensation of being prepared to defend myself, if I had to. There weren't any knights and princes coming to my rescue. Only me.

The next day I woke up with a feeling of anxiety, as if I unconsciously knew something big would happen. While Timothy was in the shower, I was on the bed, bored out of my skull. My eyes briefly glanced at his cell phone that he had left near the pillows. I don't know why exactly, but I had the curious urge to check his messages. It hadn't been the first time I'd done this. I knew many people who did the same. For me, it was a way of feeling *closer* to him. Sometimes he would talk about me behind my back to his father and later apologize, saying that they were just joking. I believe that *Curiosity* is female. I've always been a curious person. Among the many emails, my eyes fell on a letter by a certain Adriana, all in legal slang, which talked money and food for the babies. What babies? I then searched for all the other messages she had been sending him, just to understand what fresh hell was unravelling before my curious eyes. The first email between them had been written six years before we even met. The shock was horrendous... my world fell apart. There, in front of my eyes, was a whole book that revealed the backstory of Timothy's life. Judgment day had arrived. I realized that Timothy's guilty conscience and stress was due to his double life. Naturally, these awful secrets affected our own relationship. I kept peeking, as I listened out for the shower, making sure that Timothy wouldn't walk in on me. I found some photos of this lady, probably no younger than forty. She wrote that, at her age, she didn't need any money from Timothy. Even though it had been a one night stand, she would still keep the child, she wrote. There were other pictures of her with a big baby belly, requesting that he could send her some children's books. It turned out that she had twins! I wanted to strangle that lying piece of shit. I marched into the bathroom. I wanted blood. His. Fucking. Blood.

"You lousy son of a bitch!" I shouted with all the breath in my throat.

'What is it? Babe?'

I hurled the phone at Timothy's lying face, followed by any object I could get my hands on. The more I spat and screamed and cursed, the more and more he sunk to the bottom of the shower, as the water rained on him, along with my outburst.

"Twins! What the fuck?"

Although he was much bigger than me, he didn't do anything, not even when I rained some more blows down on him. Naked like a worm, he covered his head and face in his arms and sat in the corner of the shower. Not one fucking word from him. I vomited all that anger and insults I had been carrying inside me for months. It all poured out, some of it in Italian! *Mi stai prendono per il culo? Bastardo! Porca puttana! Sei cosi stronzo! Ti odio!*

If it were possible, I would have literally unscrewed the bathroom sink and fucking smashed that thing on the fucker's head. Napoli style! Once I finished, I went to the living room and threw myself on the sofa. Total silence reigned in the house. In that moment, like a wounded animal, that liar I had loved so much, entered with a towel wrapped around the hips. It was a paradoxical sight. I hated him, but at the same time he looked hot. He sat next to me with his head in his hands, crying, and asked me to forgive him.

"I never even told my parents. You don't even know how ashamed I am. I was like twenty-one. I was drunk. So drunk, you should have seen how ugly…"

"Timothy, the reality is that you're a shitty man," I replied. "You can't accept, that behind your faux respectable Catholic façade, is a fucked up guy. All that time you spent making me feel shit, making me feel inadequate as the partner of an official,' I said. "You made me dress like a nun, made me remove my hair extensions and nails, because you said that you felt like you were going out with a ten dollar stripper. You separated me from my friends. Look at you! You're just as bad. You're stained now. Get over it, officer. I'm done. I'm tired of this shit. I wonder what else you've been keeping from me. I can't trust you anymore."

He didn't know how to answer. Without a word, he got up, went to his room, got dressed and left the house. Didn't see him for days. Probably slept in his office. As for me, well, I had to go back home. I couldn't stay here. Without a penny. Without a job. Timothy returned three days later. He wasn't interested in trying to resolve the issue with me. Despite claiming that she hadn't needed money, Adriana's lawyer was now leaning on Timothy. This problem had to be resolved. It wasn't going to go away. Instead of him facing the situation responsibly, Timothy asked if I could help him, since I was more *experienced in legal matters and dramas*! Can you fucking believe that? The cheek of him made me angry, but I made the best of it, because I didn't want his money going to her. I needed it. To start again.

Firstly, I called my friend, Sarah Surai. She was an expert in international civil law, and knew stuff about cases affecting families and minors.

"Willing or not," she said, "...Timothy will have to pay! This can't be avoided."

"I get you Sarah, but you have to help him fix this, maybe they can make some agreement," I said.

Sarah explained that it would be worse if we bargained, because this woman could request alimony directly from his payslips, for up to six years. Over the years, I have learned that the best tactic is to think like the enemy. How would an enemy put a mother in a corner? An idea popped in my mind, and I immediately told my friend.

"You're evil!" she exclaimed, laughing.

I immediately wrote an email to the Canadian:

Dear Adriana,

My name is Eva. I'm Timothy's future wife. I recently discovered, with great pleasure, the deeds of my boyfriend, Father of your wonderful children. Welcome to the family!

I'm writing because we have agreed to help with the upkeep of your children. Since Timothy and I want to be part of your life, we will request shared protection from the judge. I would like to raise your children with you. It would be great to teach them Italian. What do you say?

Waiting for your cordial response.

Kind regards,
Eva

This letter was a stroke of genius. Adriana disappeared from our lives, without even responding. Now this problem was solved, there was still the question of what to do about Timothy. Meanwhile, Sienna had already returned to Italy with her father. Everyone was waiting for me.

CHAPTER 26

I T WAS THE DAY of reckoning. I casually asked Timothy to take me
back to Italy.

"Huh? You really wanna do this?! Hey, give me one last chance, will
ya? I got two tickets to Ireland. Let's go!"

I considered it as a kind of farewell trip before going back home.
I'd already made my decision. It was final. My love for Timothy was an
indescribable, sick landslide of toxic emotions but...

...Ireland had everything. It was an open bed of passion. The beautiful
views became the backdrop to our ultimate physical passions, anywhere we
found; there in the open space of the remote ponds and lakes, smothered
by an Irish forest, green with envy. Going back to the cozy hotel, with its
beautiful fireplace savaging the room, the furnace in Timothy's eyes was
making me sink back into the quicksand of our impossible relationship. I
hadn't felt this good with him since we met. Perhaps it could still work out?

As ever, my dreams of how it should've been were soon ruined by
the gunfire of reality. We hadn't been back in Germany for long, when
Timothy bounded in one day after work, happier than I've ever seen him.

"Hey! You'll never guess what? They want me to join the special forces!
Get this! In Savannah! I'm going back to America!"

Timothy loved his job more than anything else in the world. His
uniform masked the ugly, lying persona I had found frustrating; as if that
uniform itself was a super hero costume. Or maybe an invisibility cloak. I

noticed that there was a detail to his words that I didn't like. It was *I can. I want. I think. I.*

"You, or rather, us?" I asked.

His face became pale.

"You could come with me, as my official girlfriend... see if you like the place!"

I was annoyed: "Timothy, this girlfriend stuff is getting old after three fucking years! We either get married, or I go back to Italy tomorrow. I'm tired of this shit!"

"I guess I can't marry a lady who wants to put a gun to my head. I don't know if I'm ready to make that leap," he said.

The next morning I called my old friends from Vicenza who I had met during a previous move from Bamberg to Grafenwoehr. They too had found themselves caught off guard in Germany and a little depressed. They remembered me for my kindness and hospitality whenever they came to my place or if I offered them a nice lunch in a typical German restaurant. There was immediate harmony. They gave me their number, in case I might need help in the future.

Silvio answered me with his cheerfulness: "Hey, Eva! how are you? You want me to pick you up?"

I explained my situation in detail

"Okay, I understand," he said. "We're busy unloading stuff today, but since it's gonna take a while, we'll be staying here overnight. Tomorrow morning there'll be room in the truck for your stuff, so we can load it up and take it."

I knew I had no other choice. I had to take advantage of Silvio's goodwill or I'd be trapped in that life forever. That evening, I didn't even talk to Timothy. I went to bed. Early night. Timothy decided to sleep on the sofa. No goodnights.

At seven the next morning the truck arrived. Timothy was already out. I helped Silvio's boys swiftly pack the truck in case Timothy suddenly returned. I didn't want to get involved in some early morning shouting and screaming drama. We packed as fast as we could. The only problem was how to cram in the vast quanity of clothes. Gosh, I had so many outfits and shoes, but not enough boxes. I went inside to make sure I hadn't forgotten everything. The most important pieces of furniture were already on their way to Italy. I sat on the edge of the kitchen table, the only piece of furniture I hadn't shoved in the truck, and had a last look around. Every space had its own memory; special, normal, ordinary, passionate, funny, scary.

I looked triumphantly at Timothy, as soon as he returned, lost in his own apartment. It was as if a thousand ideas were running through his head at once; none of which were acceptable. Every so often there was a flash of fury in his eyes, giving way to confusion. I wasn't sure I considered a triumph, but it was what my anger needed.

Chapter 27

A MONTH LATER, I SETTLED into a new apartment that my friend Patty, a real estate agent, had managed to source. I didn't want to get involved with Timothy again, after all we had been through, but I needed a helping hand to start up again, and he was the only one I knew who would support me.

We often talked over Skype. It was strange, seeing the half empty house behind him on the grainy screen. It looked like he was lost in the machine. During one chat he said how he he wanted to meet me for one last time, before he headed off to the States. Since I needed some cash, I agreed to see him.

When he saw me, he held me tightly. His eyes were shining with tears. He then smiled, with that knowing look in his eye and motioned me towards the bedroom. I, clumsier than ever, fell for it again. Like an idiot, although I promised myself not to fall for his charms, I couldn't resist what my biology was telling me. After we finished he took the engagement ring, I had given him back, got to his knees and asked me to marry him.

"I can't expect you to go to Savannah and wait for me while I go back to Afghanistan," he said. "You can wait in Vicenza, until I come back. Then we'll go together. As man and wife."

Even though I said yes to everything, when I accompanied back to the train station, I knew in my heart that I couldn't trust him and that I probably would never see him again. He would have only broken my heart all over again.

Among the alimony from my ex-husband and a small contribution from Timothy, I was able to live fairly comfortably for a while. However, I noticed that the contributions from Timothy were beginning to diminish more and more, until one day I got a letter. I can still remember the day. It was February 17th.

Dear Eva,

I'm leaving you. I will never be the man I tried to be in your eyes, during our relationship. I loved you so much, to the point of risking everything and turning myself against everyone, just to be with you, but unfortunately today is the day for goodbyes.

You're a strong woman. If anyone can take a hit like this, I guess it's you. I wish I could say the same for myself. This is gonna hit me real hard. I've also decided not to send you any more money, because I know you, and I know that money will never be enough for you...

In those cold and hard words, the sense of romance that had existed between us vanished. It was as if we hadn't shared anything special. I thought of all those things that I had lost, including my time, which I could never get back. I thought of all the pain that guy put me through, with his lies and illusions. That bastard had placed a scar on my soul. Nevertheless, I was pervaded by a kind of relief. I replied with the same coldness, saying that at least he could have left me with a 'gift', since I had lost the house tmy ex had left me.

Dear Timothy,

It's not my fault that you wanted a trophy wife. You're too cheap for it. I accepted you for better and *worse*. I've lost everything. You must be a magician of the dark arts, sweetie, because you sure transformed my pure love into a *fierce hatred.*

You always hid behind your little finger, with all your "Oh, I'm fucked up". If anything, it's you who has fucked me up. What you wrote is like a spit in the face! You could have just helped me out, like a gentleman; as a tribute to what I meant to you, but no…you treat me like a gypsy.

You will get what you deserve.

Eva

His response was immediate:

Hey!

I know you will have your revenge. I don't think I deserve it, but there's nothing I can do about it. My life was over the day I met you. It was the biggest mistake I've ever made but hey, I'll deal with that when it happens.

Timothy

I almost felt sorry for him. I was tempted to let him go, as if he had put a loaded gun in my hand, to give him the coup de grace. I decided to think about it. Let him stew.

CHAPTER 28

RAUL WAS ONE OF the few friends I had left in the military world; everyone else had gone back to America and some had died in battle. Raul had unfortunately lost a leg, but he was nevertheless a fascinating man with Indian features, a powerful complexion, and the will to live. It's an odd admission but that stump of his made him seem sexy. He was the sunniest person in this world. Whenever I was in his presence I felt serene.

While the farce with Timothy was over, I still couldn't accept the feeling that I had used like all the common bed warmers I had known before. The experience still hurt me and I couldn't let it go. I had to take sedatives to help with the sleepless nights of stress, worry, hurt and anger. One day Raul, who could see that something was eating me up, looked at me and said: "Eva, we have to remove this pain of yours. Tell me, what would make you the happiest in this world right now? I'm going to Tel Aviv this weekend. Do you want to come with me?"

I was immersed in my thoughts.

"Sorry? Oh yeah, right...I just need some clousure with something or I'll never be able to go forward."

Raul nodded. "I get you, yeah. What would you like?"

"I want to be myself. That's all I've ever wanted. I can't stand the shame of how stupid and gullible I was. I don't think I could accept another woman taking my place in the life he had planned with me! If another woman ever loves him, it will be because she loves the real Timothy, not that liar who only wears that uniform to man up! He will probably only find happiness selling cars or being a mailman. And she will have the man I never had! He must feel the pain of losing everything, just as I did!"

The next morning, with a fierce determination in my eyes, I took that famous little USB from when I had uploaded information when I lived with him. I went to a bookshop and printed everything that was on it. Once the file was ready, I showed up at the military court at the base that had, only a couple of years previously, investigated the inappropriate affair we were having, during my divorce. The same colonel who had investigated the case, had told me at the time:

"Madam, you are an accomplice of an individual who is offending the honor of the American Army! He is lacking in morality and in open violation of the rules. He is a liar and unreliable man. If you fail to take the right action, you are on his level."

Those words had been branded on my mind all these years. I also had a nightmarish, maybe irrational fear, that the death of one of our second lieutenant friends in Afghanistan, had been due to Timothy's irresponsible selfishness. Perhaps it was paranoia, due to riding the emotional rollercoaster in and out of hell. It was difficult to explain and rationalise but it persisted. It was only a feeling, but I couldn't stop wondering that if we had never got together in the first place, and I hadn't played this stupid game of love in Germany, perhaps that soldier would have still been alive today. Perhaps it was fate.

I left the material with the same colonel, who was still working at the same office. He grinned as he fingered the pile of documents. "Well, it's sure been awhile but you've made the right choice. Thanks."

I was unable to reply, except with a melancholic smile. When I went home that night, for the first time in months, I was able have a restful night's sleep. I didn't get involved in the process, but I eventually discovered from a couple of the soldiers' wives that he was dishonorably discharged from the army.

CHAPTER 29

I T WAS OFTEN MY male friends who helped me climb the career ladder. Gianluca, a friend and established journalist, found me a little job as a commentator for a TV channel in Padua. It felt strange being back in front of the cameras, but as a woman and mother I finally felt accepted and lived up to the role. I had so many interesting experiences on that panel show, discussing the issues of the day and sharing opinions.

One time they invited an intellectual, an Italian general, and the Mayor of Verona. Gianluca had placed so much trust in me, that I didn't want to disappoint him. I nodded intelligently at all the things they said, making sure to show my best profile for the cameras. I wondered if the audience at home could understood what they were talking about because I sure didn't have a clue. All of a sudden the Mayor of Verona addressed me. I was taken aback.

"And you, Signorina! Do you have any ideas about what we could do for a city like Verona?"

At that moment something occurred to me. When I returned from Germany and was desperately looking for work in Verona, I remembered seeing the statue of Juliet being pawed and molested like a sex toy, by thousands of disrespectful tourists in front in the eyes of my child.

I replied with a snappy comeback.

"We could start by putting a statue of Romeo next to Juliet, so we can fondle his crotch, too!" I said this in my most bimbo voice, but dry as a bolt from the blue. It was necessary to give them a show, no? At least I got it off my chest. Wherever we go, in any big city, we see people, monuments and statues being molested by tourists. We see lakes and canals being used like trash cans and grand steps used as a toilets. The presenter and the guests were shocked at first by my straight talk. Then they started laughing, thinking I was only joking. No. I explained my point.

"Basically, whenever I take my daughter to see the beauties in Verona, I have to constantly explain why everybody is assaulting that particular statue. What's the deal? What am I supposed to say to her? 'Hey, honey, Juliet loves having strangers mauling her breasts?!' If we need to be so embarassing, then, let's go for the full course! Equal opportunities. Put Romeo there. Romeo and Juilet. Fondle them both or remove Juliet!"

I continued to bounch the ball back to the pitcher. After all, I was having fun, which was rare during these transmissions. The Mayor, however, offered his support, instead of attacking me, perhaps he wanted to make women understand that he too cared about equal opportunities.

"Wonderful idea, but we can't remove Juliet. It's a great tourist attraction that brings a lot of income to the city! However, since your idea is fun and useful, I offer my commitment to authorize such a project, in a place chosen by you, if you can find yourself someone to mold a statue."

A handshake sealed the deal. Soon I would also have an official document in my hands. The problem was: how could I get a statue of that kind made? My experience in public relations would help, but this time I also needed a bit of luck.

Chapter 30

THE FIRST PIECE FELL into place in Naples. I was at the station cafeteria, ordering a coffee) for me and my mother, when I felt instantly observed. I'd only been back a few minutes, from Ischia, where I had spent a pleasant day at the beach with the children. Obviously, I wasn't in my usual diva outfit.

I turned and saw a well-built southerner, with thick, black hair, and a shabby beard, but in a good way. The open shirt, from where the hairy chest was peeking, made him look quite hot. His natural tan highlighted his green eyes. My God, he looked cool! I smiled at him with my usual security, but I had to turn around because I was almost giggling. It had been a while since a man had looked at me with such interest. I'm used to being stared at by men. It can lift my spirits. It doesn't usually bother me. I'm in control. I set the limits of what I find acceptable. If I don't like a particular man's attention, it only takes my swift, dangerous glance, to make him avert his eyes and stare at his girl, instead of me. Still, with this guy, I almost felt kidnapped by his interest. What was he doing to me in his mind? It was, I have to say, fascinating! Who was this guy? Maybe luck had decided to knock on my door.

"Miss, can I offer you a coffee?" he asked me, in a way that already assumed that I would accept.

"Well, let's see. Since I'm going to sit at the table, would you bring me two coffee, please? We're over there, behind the column," I replied in a tone that had no objections.

Who knew what he was thinking? He probably thought that I was with a friend; two bored tourists with their children; waiting for summer to arrive. No big plans. His smile, as beautiful as the sun, found me at the table; while Sienna was quarrelling with her grandmother. "I'm Riccardo!" he announced. He laugh boomed loudly as he had coffee with us. It was nice to know that this classic southern gigolò, was actually an exquisite person with a heart of gold. He was also a sculptor of some fame, as I discovered while chatting to him.

Riccardo was well-known in Italy. He was also working on a few international projects. I knew then that he would be the best person for the idea I had in mind. He decided there and then to collaborate with me on my Juliet project. He already had sponsors in mind, who would jump at the chance of exploring such an ingenious and original idea. He was one of the few people I'd met who understood how commitment and good intentions must be poured into an idea.

Two months later, Riccardo called to tell me the good news. He had managed to get me an invitation for a massively important sponsored exhibition of modern art; organised by a well-known company that provided marble for the sculptures. I was amazed that the elegant style of the company had good taste and pleasantly surprised to see so many faces I knew. I hadn't known that they shared my interest in art. The best part of this show was watching the sculptors, carving brand new gorgeous statues before our astonished eyes. Riccardo, covered in marble dust, was putting on a show for the guests. I was so fixated watching him model the hard rock with such mastery; dominating the scene; that I didn't notice the nice middle-aged gentleman at my side. The little gentleman turned out to be a man called Silvio; one of the most succesful industrialists in the Veneto region. I was amused as I listened to him, because he spoke almost only in Venetian dialect and from a mile away I could see that he did not disdain the company and intelligence of beautiful women. He already knew who I was and what I was doing there.

"Eva, Riccardo explained the project to me. If you're serious, I'll give you the sponsorship. No fooling around. I only take on projects I believe in. I recommend you take my offer because I don't put my nose in any old project, for anyone, unless I get results."

It was hard to believe that, for once in my life, things were flowing with ease. That evening's party was splendid. All evening we drank prosecco and toasted our futures. I wasn't just happy just because the project was taking form, but also because finally, after many years kicking and screaming, I began to feel that men were treating me with due respect. This of course increased my strength and my self-esteem...

...even my new marriage was turning a bed of roses! That year I met Adam, the man of my life. I owe it to all my haters that I met this fantastic man; this true love of mine; this American Beauty; this American smile sculpted onto the face of a Prince. He believed in me when others wanted to give up. After I had destroyed my ex-boyfriend's career and dreams, local newspapers couldn't wait a second to write about what happened. I had almost missed their 'friendly fire'. Not long after I had met Adam, he told me that one day he was peeking my photos on Facebook when a passing waiter stopped and exclaimed: "Beware of that woman! She is dangerous. You're gonna be ruined!"

Adam still reminds me that this was the time he fell in love with me and wanted to get to know me at *all costs*. Risk and danger are games for real men. Adam fell into the criteria of a *real man*. Instead of trying to hurt me, by trying to steer men away from me, people only succeed, in pushing them closer to me. I wonder what these fear-mongers and jealous tongues would say to this. How could a wonderful paratrooper ever be afraid of my blue eyes? Blue like the sky he jumped out of. That was how Adam jumped into my arms. Into my Earth. Into our sacred Garden of Eden.

CHAPTER 31

Back in Verona there were some problems brewing. I wouldn't say that the mayor was a friend exactly, but certainly a great supporter of the project. Unfortunately, I made a massive miscalculation; for neither me nor the mayor had taken into account the plethora of gray bureaucrats who lurked around the palace. They weren't only skeptical of the idea, which went against the Veronese tradition, but they were also super biased towards me; as a woman and a professional. I didn't expect there to be such a retrograde mentality; that people could be annoyed seeing me so close to the mayor.

It wasn't long before they started nitpicking the project, to find every way they could to frustrate the process and slow it down. No-one had the balls to openly face the mayor, or speak out against a project on women's rights, but they invented every possible quibble to frustrate me. There were days when everything and everyone almost succeeded in demotivating me, but the thing I had set in motion was bigger than me, and I couldn't disappoint all those people who where working their asses off 24/7 to finish the project. Unfortunately, the gray minions won the first round. In fact, they managed to procrastinate so long, that the elections for a new mayor had already arrived. Naively, I thought that this election would help me. The new council, I dreamed, would dust away those petty bureau bugs and give the administration fresh blood to start anew. Instead I discovered that the bureaucrats had their asses nailed to the chair. Given the preconceived hostility towards me, I no longer believed that it was about a principle but what was *practical*. They just couldn't hack the fact that what I was offering to Verona, was something they hadn't considered. I wanted to breath equal and modern life into that crazy city, (the Italians often call the Veronese *i tutti matti*). People had it set into their gray skulls that I was only motivated by destruction and danger, but here I was offering creation, hope and life to Verona.

The Save Juliet project had its expenses well within its budget by the company in Chiampo, who were eagerly supporting me. The municipality of Verona was not expected to shell out a penny or lift a finger, as my team were doing all the work. As if this wasn't enough, an old classmate of mine also joined the project. Since school, he had become a brilliant app programmer and expert in microchips. Unfortunately for him, due to his looks (like a nerd from the 80s), nobody took him too seriously. Also he was in some deep shit, as some of the projects he was involved weren't really going anywhere. I decided first thing to introduce him to various friends with plenty of cash who needed smart people.

Around the same time, a letter suddenly arrived from the town hall in Verona, in which I was told blandly that the Save Juliet project was no longer in line with the contingent needs of the city and, as a consequence, the administrators were no longer interested. It was such a low-down shameful mockery, after almost two years going back and forth, but I wasn't ready to give up yet.

I was in the car with Carlo, the super nerd, when had a stroke of genuine inspiration.

"Eva, we have to go to the new mayor with an original idea that's beyond anyone's expectations. Something that doesn't just contain a message, but also carries a novelty value for tourism; something futuristic. Like, a cybernetic statue! I could easily create a microchip to insert inside the statue of Romeo. Tourists could then use a special app, and with those new Google glasses, there could be a chance to see all information in augmented realty!"

I beamed. This kid was a fricking nerd but wow!

"Imagine it Eva! We'd be able to beam holograms of all the historical people from the past, like Juliet on the balcony! Like weird ghosts or something!"

The more we talked, the more we felt inspired, and ideas flowed with incredible fludity. Therefore I decided to add this substantial technological aspect to the project, and propose it directly to the mayor. Once I could get in that damn place!

I had to get in like a wrecking ball, because those pen-pushing bureau rats were trenching themselves not to give me an inch; so I called Verona newspapers and told them about my odyssey with the town hall. Someone from the newspaper contacted the mayor. I already imagined his response. He hadn't the faintest idea who this young lady from Vicenza was, but saw no reason to set up a meeting.

The great day of meeting with the new mayor eventually came.

He wasn't what I expected. I hadn't really been paying attention to the recent elections. I expected someone to greet me who looked like most mayors; gray, sad, middle-aged, smart but bland. This mayor was young, tall and very elegant. It was a pleasant surprise because at least it meant that this young mayor would be receptive to modern ideas. Obviously, I took Carlo with me, because I would never have been able to explain that whole nerdy jargon myself. The mayor seemed immediately interested. If at the beginning he thought I were just another PR, with lame, cliched ideas, by the time I had finished, he was convinced of the goodness of the project. He was also interested in the technological aspect, as it could be applied to other monuments. He didn't refuse the idea offhand. He told me it could be very interesting, but before it could be taken further, it was necessary to select the area where the statue could be located. The only discordant note, was that it was only gentleman's agreement at this stage. There weren't any papers or contracts involved, so I had to trust this handsome man.

When we left the building, Carlo smiled and said. "It was a productive meeting. I was so proud of you in there, Eva! You spoke calmly but with so much passion. Thanks for inviting me. I'm glad someone appreciates what I do."

Time passed. Summer came and went. Everything slowed down. Carlo had also vanished into thin air. If I had to explain my project, how in the world could I talk about apps and virtual reality, without sounding like a dork? I would look like some kinda snakeoil woman. I was desperate too, because the company I represented were getting flaky and didn't appreciate the bad publicity. When I finally managed to trace this nerd, through the phone of Katya, one of my coworkers, I immediately started storming him with questions, so much so that he defensively but, with a guilty conscience, warned me not even to mention our collaboration to anyone. I then discovered that the ungrateful virgin had succeeded, through another acquantance, to secure massive funds for another project, and tossed me aside like an old brick, without even having the balls to admit it. I felt so fucked up. Naturally, I gave him a cold piece of my mind.

The whole story of Juliet was given another blast of fresh air and hope, when months later, during a political event in Vicenza, I met an assistant who worked with the Mayor of Verona. I made a brief summary of the whole Juliet story. He listened intently and was both impressed and sympathetic with my plight, to get this thing green lit. He said that he would do all that he could, in his power, to make my project happen.

Too bad then, that a few weeks later, this *assistant* of the mayor made me relive the nightmare and shame of being an independent, business woman; treating me like some air-headed good time girl. He littered my inbox with messages, informing me that he was also married. He invited my friends and I out with him, without our respective partners, to party and have *fun*. It was terrible. Naturally I didn't entertain his creepy invitations. I thought how depressing and predictable it was. Is it possible, in this world, to meet and do business with anyone, anymore, without them wanting to use the body for ejaculation practise? Can't anyone explore creative projects without impurity? Does there always have to be a hidden agenda? Many women know the answers to these questions. I sometimes dream of the days before instant communication. WhatsApp /Facebook, it seems, doesn't encourage communication and friendship, but destroys it. Social Media is nothing more than a loaded gun. We only have to open the newspapers and read all the stories about lives and relationships that have been destroyed by instant gratification. We read them avidly. We rub our hands. We say 'ooh'. We can't get enough of the gossip, because we're social and curious creatures, but under all the words, in between the lines, we can't see the devastation and emotional debris.

Resigned, I decided to abandon the project.

I thought about the children I was raising and billions of mothers all over the world; who wanted to give their kids the best start and the best education, but were unable to because of these kind of men, who want to use women like dogs. I even resisted the temptation to let this creep's wife read the messages I saved.

Nothing would have changed. Forgive me, Juliet.

CHAPTER 32

I T WAS HARD TO admit that I lost the battle for Juliet. Instead I decided to lose myself in the loving affection of my children and husband. This is the only 'loss' which feels like a victory.

One morning, as I was getting out of bed, I found Adam fully immersed on Facebook. He didn't look very amused. I took a quick look at the page he was looking at. Some page called Confessions. Still sleepy, I shrugged my shoulders and went to get myself a coffee. When I returned to our room, he was still there. What exactly was peaking his interest? My husband has never particularly been a social animal on the computer. He's a gamer. A competitor. A player. A winner. I looked a little closer at the page but, apart from the large number of participants (about four thousand), I really couldn't put my finger on what was so alluring.

"Hey, why you wanna waste the whole morning on Facebook?"

"Nothing, some guys told me about this group. I wanted to scope it out, see what it was about," he answered with his usual calm, "...but these confessions look nothing more like some slut shaming by a bunch of frustrated Blue Bar losers," he added. We read some of the posts together. At first we laughed. How could people waste so much time with dull gossip and insults? Daft, silly things. Over time, these messages went from ridicule to the libellous. People I knew, and deeply respected, were called names like pedophile, whore, drug addict. And there was even less laughter when, out of the blue, the messages, took on a darker, personal tone. Some messages were insulting *me*, even threatening me with death. What the fuck was going on?

Someone had clearly been stalking me on my Facebook page, and in real life, since the messages contained information about my every move inside the American base. I was certain these anonymous comments were also sent by employees of the base, because certain information was too detailed to be written by some bored soccer mom with plenty of time on her hands.

If in previous times, I had been simply baffled by the baseness of libellous comments against me, this time I was seriously worried. The anger from these cowards gnawed at me inside. If I had at least known who they were, I would have got them by their ears and, one by one, and dragged these fuckers to court, but none of these keyboard warriors was bold enough to write their real names. What was even more disgusting, while the comments were anonymous and debasing, were the people who tapped 'like' or posted a comment; which appeared as a notification. I was pretty dismayed. I checked the profiles of these people who enjoyed the posts, as I was curious to see who the hell was 'liking' these death threats and slut-shaming. Perhaps they were some kind of alt-right rednecks, misplacing their rage, or 'show-biz' people trying to get some visibility for their failing Facebook pages. No.

They were almost *all women* from twenty-five to forty; wives of soldiers and proud mums! Not only that. In their profiles, they regularly published images of *Our Lord the Redeemer*, or their sweet little ones struggling with the potty. I never expected that these virtuous housewives had so much anger inside, or that I could have done anything to deserve their outbursts. This infernal game got worse by the month. It was useless continuing to file a complaint against some anonymous geeky dickhead, since with Facebook's policy on privacy, there's very little that even the military command can do. Or so they told me. So I decided that I would investigate alone, to see if I could at least find the administrator of the page.

I had a suspicion. There was this guy called Benny, a well known veteran at the base in Vicenza for more than twelve years; married to a woman with quite a bad rep, so much so that she had become pregnant by another man and had left her poor husband. This same character and his other half had created a similar page like this before, with the only important difference that the posts were not at all anonymous, and therefore punishable by law. In the past I had also reported them to authority, which resulted in the page being closed. Months later, the Confessions page was started up with a special feature: it allowed anonymous posts, and was impossible to punish people. The signs all pointed to this time waster, also known for being quite a troublemaker. Along with my sister and a couple of friends, we did an experiment. We anonymously published burning and truthful details about the infidelity of his wife (she never divorced beccause she didn't want to lose bridal benefits of a veteran). These posts, sent by four different sources, were strangely never published. It was clear by now that, if it wasn't really him, there was no firm evidence that it was anyone else either.

I tried not to turn this into a personal drama and got on with my life. Although I was the favorite target of that group of bullies, anybody could be a victim. I heard that a Private, whom I had met already a couple of times was ill with depression. He wound up reading terrible things about himself and his illness. Then, the same evening, he left a suicide note, where he wrote these exact words:

True, bad things have happened to me in my life, but it's nothing compared to what I have experienced in here. There is darkness in this community. Too many secrets, polluting every corner of this place. I find it hard to believe that so much evil can exist in one place, and to make things even more difficult, so many of us remain isolated, with not even the least support from others.

No one really knows what happens in our lives, in our heart, in our minds. I wonder if that's the case everywhere, or if it's just here. I want to go. I would never kill myself, but I want to die every day. I ask God to take me in a natural way, into the last slumber. And I don't know if this is wrong or if it's how He planned it, but I know that I cry more than I eat or sleep. I had never experienced depression like this. I arrived here, without knowing what pain was, not even physical pain. Even if they (the military leaders) tell us that there is support and we can request it, it is not acceptable to be weak, and I would be treated like an infected person. For this reason we hide our pain, and we feel alone. Our smile does not mean we're fine. Take a moment to watch us in the eyes, you will see a broken soul, and some of us silently pray to be saved, but most of the time nobody listens to us, until it's too late.

The post was sent to me by a dear friend of mine, Sofia, who constantly followed that disgusting page, and was also very worried about how they treated me.

"I see bad omens," she told me one day.

The following morning, the whole community came to know of the suicide of that poor teen Private in his dorm. How it happened was classified information, but I immediately ran to see if the post was still on the page, to report the matter. Luckily my friend sent me the screenshot, because there was no trace anywhere of that tragic letter. I felt almost guilty, not being able to save that poor kid. Maybe I should have insisted more, made some desperate gesture. My husband consoled me, explaining that unfortunately depression is a more common evil in the army than what we think, and that the Confessions page was was just the last straw. I promised myself that I would do everything possible to denounce that rotten system. No longer should more people have to suffer because of these toxic pages and the cowards and evil bullies that shrank behind them.

Still having several contacts among the national mass media, I didn't waste a second spreading the message that bullying, far from being silly gossip to pass the time, had now become a dangerous and criminal system, and the death of that boy and the depression of others were on the consciences of Facebook, the army and the Media. The next day it was clear I kicked a hornet's nest and released a haze of anger. I had destroyed an anthill too, and the ants went crazy, once they realized that I would no longer use my 'bimbo' manners, but was ready to go *medieval*. Base commanders hated getting involved with national newspapers and television stations. They sure didn't appreciate a light being shone in their faces or negative publicity about their incompetence. Why should anyone object to keeping people safe? Sure beats the hell outta me.

CHAPTER 33

'BEST FRIEND' IS AN expression that's sometimes difficult to understand, especially in the female world. Roxanne arrived at the right time; a beautiful Sunday afternoon at the Golf Club in Asiago. I was pregnant with my second child.

This beautiful red-haired Texan stopped at my table and asked me if we had already met somewhere before. I was a little scared at first. I was a bit touchy because you know, the pregnancy and all deep shit the petty military community had been causing. I was weary of her kind smile. Roxanne still laughs as she remembers how I looked like a cat, spitting at its opponent. After some time observing her and studying her (which I always do with people I first meet) I felt that she was actually a well meaning person. When she sat down next to me and ordered a coffee, I wasn't the least bit disturbed. I even remember that she embraced me.

"Sorry if I reacted a little badly," I explained. "I guess it's a bit of everything."

I starting telling her about how my life, about Juliet's abandoned project and the torment which I was subjected to by the anonymous assholes, who were trying to hurt me and Adam. Roxanne was pleasantly surprised I was able to open up like this spontaneously. We found we had many things in common. Roxanne was a different kind of person in this environment she stood out in away that gave them fear. The kind of fear that is deep in someone's soul because they see a truth teller. Roxanne had never stepped away from a burning flame she looked into the belly of the fire and went inside even when she was threatened with lashing flames. We would later discover that these truths would bring us great obstacles nothing we could imagine. She explained that the base was a toxic environment all around; soldiers and civilians were suffering alike, she always had hope for justice though and vowed to always help. These idealistic views would be tested and tried, we would later reflect on how much light we had in the truth. There had already been some investigations on real or alleged abuses of power, but the only thing that was certain, was the corruption, both moral and economic, which was plaguing the place; as chronyism and nepotism ran amock.

This was the start of our friendship. Cast in stone.

CHAPTER 34

AT LONG LAST THERE was a friendly and fun ally in that swamp. A sweet, middle-aged gentleman. A mild-mannered guy with a kind and traditional elegance. He appeared to me as an angel, who had arrived to save me from a life of drudgery and envy, that were the *"caserma"—army base.*

Whenever I talked to him about my cat, or his hometown, or where I was going on vacation, I finally felt accepted and respected by the community. In his company, I found it easy to forget about gossip. He also invited me to mass at the base, and explained the activities of the church, the beauty of sincere faith, and how close he was to God. Perhaps he thought I was a lost sheep. Up until then, I was only really going to the base for groceries and the gym, before running back home to my family. Although this guy wasn't the only American I was comfortable with, he was certainly the only one I could talk to about everything. With him, I could chat about international politics, or his adventures around the world, with extreme ease.

One day there was Facebook request. But who was that grizzled man, so adventurous and sporty? I didn't even realize the request was from the guy who had been talking to me about God's grace and eternal patience. Indeed, to tell you the truth, he was one of those forgettable aquaintances you meet at the gym, every now and again, who you might talk to, but forget to ask their name. I didn't know that this guy was army general! Now I could see why he exuded such confidence; such an Alpha male. I had in fact noticed that people were quite respectful towards him at the gym, but I thought it was just for his natural charm. There was no way I expected him to add me on Facebook at eleven in the evening!

"You are the girl who always smiles."

As I read this, I knew it was him. The General. In fact, he always left me with the phrase *keep smiling*. It was a boring Friday night, it was raining out and I just had quarrel with my husband, because of that bitchy hag of his sister! I found out she'd been influenced from the bad comments on the Confessions page and had started to bad mouth me!

Sometimes, I wonder if Adam's family had a soft spot for me. They love their children so much. In the past, they always had bad experiences with the previous husbands of their daughter, Felicia. So, I thought that maybe they were expecting adverse surprises from their children's lovers.

Yet, it still does not change the fact that I disliked how their daughter disgraced and defamed me on social media. I was very sad to know that my husband's parents tolerated the doings of their daughter and that they did nothing to stop her. I was even angry with my husband because I felt like he was not standing up for me. But I realized that the love for one's own children or siblings always comes first.

To unwind, I agreed to chat with the General. I needed to vent to someone; anyone; and so I told him about everything that my husband's family were putting me through, and how I thought that my man hadn't been defending me as much as I expected. I guess later I could see that he'd been placed into a difficult situation between his family and me, but that evening, I just needed to calm down. I was so engrossed in this conversation, I didn't notice that, as we finished, it was two in the morning.

The fateful third year of our marraige had arrived, unfortunately, when beautiful, brilliant, sky-diving passion isn't enough to forget about the other's flaws. Cultural differences also began to become an issue. I was the daughter of entrepreneurs from Veneto, and Adam was from a family of blue collars in Ohio. In addition, he had left home much later than I did, and this too had a great influence on how we saw the world. Having both suffering from hard vibes from life, we couldn't always communicate our problems clearly to each other. He used to shell himself up in his own silence, watching a movie and pretending the day after, that nothing had happened. However I don't forget. I accumulate negativity. I hid these concerns of mine to my loved ones. This was my 'third' marriage and I wasn't even thirty. Since my previous relationships had also failed because of my impulsiveness, this time I didn't want to leave anything to chance. Adam was *worth it*. Not only was he a very handsome man, but also very sincere and *genuine*. I needed to be certain that my children had a father of whom be proud. How could I reconcile my almost pathological allergy to boredom with all the duties of a family life? I've always had this issue and I guess it's something I'm dealing with, but back then I felt that I was becoming trapped in a pantomime again, and it seemed like the people I cared about only expected me to be a good housewife.

That was how my friendship with the general began; ironically, right on those same toxic social networks that had given me so many issues. I needed a secret friend. The general and I had become some kind of logbook to each other; a kind of private diary. In the evening I was used to sleeping late, while my husband, had to get up to go to work in the dark of the night. When I had finished my business, I often had hours of solitude that I now filled with our chitchats. I did not feel guilty. I was at peace with myself because I had no second goals, and hidden agendas. I only wanted a moment of leisure, far away from the 'tragedies' of the world and my personal quarrels. Our dialogues were different from what people would expect. These chats continued for a few weeks.

Where are you tonight? I asked.

In Mozambique, training the police against corruption, he replied.

How is it over there? I've always been intrigued by Africa! I would love to visit the Sahara, I commented.

Unfortunately I don't have much time for safaris, but look at this!

(Here he sent me a picture of the beautiful view from his hotel room)

However I prefer the animals from gym, especially the *lionesses*, he wrote one day.

I didn't give it too much importance at the beginning, even if it wouldn't have been the first time he wrote something like that. Some "toxic masculinity", in small doses, is to be expected, even from the best of men. If I'm honest, I was a little amused, and so I answered in kind.

Too bad you like lionesses, I wrote, because I see myself like a *cheetah*, the fastest and most difficult to take.

For me, the question could be solved this way. He would tell a joke and I would put it back in its place. I liked these kind of games and so I played along to a certain extent. I felt like it was like trying to tame a tiger, or rather a lion, since he considered himself to be the king of the jungle.

Aren't you afraid of the generals? Are you a Russian spy by any chance? he asked.

I don't fear men whatsoever, I responded.

I told him about that whole affair with that politician, who almost raped me years ago. I then asked if he believed in friendship between man and woman. He replied that he loved the strength of women and sent me several photos with him and important VIP women, even the one he took with the Queen of England, to make me understand what kind of women he liked to be associated with.

I felt intoxicated because it seemed that I, like these powerful women, was strong enough to tame this man; frozen in his role but still looking for an escape. I deluded myself into believing that my way of answering him in a smooth and dry way would have kept him at bay, but this only seemed to release his giant ego.

I had a favor to ask him. I explained to him about those awful Facebook pages, which had been such a pain in the ass for me and Adam. So he decided to show me that he wasn't just a big fart, but had power in the real world. In a week, that Confessions page with four thousand people, disappeared from the face of the earth. The administrator of that page, a person working inside the base, was fired with no further explanation.

I was ecstatic.

CHAPTER 35

FINALLY IT SEEMED THE winds were finally in our sails. Mostly on my husband's side, as he too had to fight to take the full weight of that barrage of lies and harassments.

Unfortunately, things then went in a different direction than I had expected. I was used to men flirting with me. Sometimes they were in the harsh manners of some guests during television broadcasts, or in the ironic fashion, like my friends. When the General started flirting, it seemed somewhat out of character, but I didn't give it any weight. I told Adam about my friendship with a general of the base, without naming names. He didn't need to know everything about our conversations, as there was nothing that I couldn't handle. He was just relieved that that awful Facebook page had been shutdown. My husband always appreciated my social skills. It was a quality he admired. We were so in love, that there was no room for immature jealousies, so he never asked me for the details of my chat with the General.

Being a very closely knit environment, my husband's colleagues would tell him everything; every time they saw me in the gym, chatting with the General of the base. This wasn't considered as becoming for military wives. Even exchanging a high five was almost sacrilegious. I didn't care about it, because I wasn't a military woman. I had nothing to hide. Besides, I thought they were just making their petty, scornful remarks, because the 'special friendship' I had with their boss. They were inventing a scandal that didn't exist. My husband actually found it amusing the first few times. But after a while, the pressure of his colleagues was so heavy, that he asked me to stop talking to the General, and said that I should stop the friendship here and now. I almost frowned. The General had, I thought, our best interests and well-being at heart. However, after almost four months of conversations, he began to call me on messenger and video; especially while my husband was on a mission abroad. Even then it seemed innocent. We talked about our children, who happened to be in class together. One evening, he called me because he was feeling bad, having eaten something rotten, in some village in Africa. He was like a frightened child who thought he had been poisoned. When he called later me that night at two, telling me that he had just vomitted his stomach up, I began to worry. Why was he calling me and not his wife? I started to worry what would happen if he felt something for me and reacted badly if I rejected any advance he wanted to make. Espeically after he had proved himself vulnerable to me. I thought about it and decided that I should speak to him, face to face, so he could see there was no malice and hard feelings in my eyes. I invited him for coffee at the base cafe 'Da Gino', but he said that it wasn't a good idea, so I replied we could go downtown, but he replied that it was even worse, because whenever he left the base, he was escorted by twelve carabinieri, who never left him alone.

He called me one day and suggested that I could go and see him at his house, since his wife was in America, visiting relatives. I declined the invitation, explaining that I couldn't justify visiting his home, out of respect for my husband. I understood that things were getting bad when he confessed that he'd been thinking about me while he was in the shower. I had to work out how to try to end our secret friendship in a smooth manner. I was so sorry because I loved his intelligence and sympathy. I wish we could have remained friends, with no string attached. Losing his 'protection' risked hurting Adam too. It was sure turning into a fine mess. I had to come up with an excellent idea. The proverbial feminine touch came to my aid.

"Why not organize a small show with your press office in Venice, with the Italian authorities of the base?" I asked him. "Harry's Bar is a beautiful little place for the privileged people, and I know the owners. I will be there 'by chance'. You told me that you would have to organize it soon anyway, so let's kill two birds with one stone."

It took him a week to do the paperwork. After all, he too was in a hurry to leave both problems behind, unaware that I wanted to end the interesting but unbearable friendship.

CHAPTER 36

THAT DAY HAD ARRIVED, and frankly I was also feeling very lively and amused. I've always loved taking the water taxi to see my favorite city.

I arrived with my little white Dolce and Gabbana dress and an elegant camel coat. My 12 cm *tacchi dodici* never lets me down, even in the Venetian narrow cobble streets. I was lucky because I ran into some friends at Harry's; Franco the owner of a famous hotel I had often stayed at during the 'single' phase of my life and Gerva; a Venetian nobleman who, during the 80s had been one of the most famous Italian playboys, who 'scouted' for actresses for the Film Festival. The bar was, as usual, full, but two tables had been reserved for us. Franco and Gerva were about to leave and settle the bill. When they saw me, they decided to stay a little longer and invite me to take a mimosa or two, and talk about old times; like the time Gerva had appeared at a party at Cipriani's with Brad Pitt and George Clooney, leaving all of us dropping our jaws.

From the outside, they looked like a nice group of tourists, but tourists don't enter a bar almost goose stepping. While watching this scene, it intoxicated me to think that I was the one who had put everything into motion. How easy it was to manipulate power, with little feminine charm and common sense. The General sat down, as expected, but he didn't lose an opportunity to send me significant side looks. After a while, I apologised to my friends. I got up, pretending I had to go to the bathroom, but eventually came to the counter, where I was now alone. It was comical, because the General started to act as if he were surprised to see me, while his guests were preparing to start eating, regardless of him. The General came over and offered me a drink.

Our meeting was significant, I said. I had a way of explaining things from my point of view, without any misunderstanding. I was very keen on our crazy friendship I said, but that was all I wanted, a mere friendship with no strings attached, because I loved my husband very much. He replied with grace, that he too loved his wife, but that the solitude at the top of the command was such a burden. He also loved my rebellious life and my stories. Always surrounded by responsibility and accompanied everywhere by his escort, he had found a happy shelter in our friendship, where he didn't always have to behave as a husband or general. I was glad he told me that. Things seemed clear, and I felt almost flattered by his kind words, but relieved that we could slowly back away from this 'dangerous friendship.'

Until I opened Messenger.

He told me how happy he'd been to see me. He hoped that he would see me again soon. At his home.

I understood then that he was either intentionally oblivious, or else... I couldn't say, but the kind of friendship that I thought bounded us was done. It was difficult to cut that bond for good. Don't ask me why, I can't even explain it to myself. I just needed a trusted friend in that cage of fools and stalkers, not another horny dog who was thinking of getting laid. I'm not exactly a mormon gal, but it seems that everyone misunderstands my uninhibited nature for something else. Mindful of previous experiences, each time he asked me to delete our conversations, I did the exact opposite, and it was my salvation.

CHAPTER 37

ONE AFTERNOON, I WAS walking under the rain, without an umbrella. I'd been to the gym when I noticed an elegant lady in the distance, coming towards me. She wasn't carrying umbrella but carrying an attitude. If looks could kill, I'd have been dead on the spot. When she passed, I wondered who the hell that was.

A memory sparkled in my mind. I had seen that beautiful woman before on Facebook. Besides Henry. The General. It couldn't have been anyone other than his wife. Strangely, that evening he did not write to me. Since I was a little unnerved by her presence and a little surprised by his silence, I wrote to him.

I think I've met your sweet wife but she didn't seem too happy to see me. She looked at me in a threatening way, I wrote.

Don't worry, she has this authoritarian way about her, he responded.

I paused. Perhaps he thought all blonds were air-heads. There was something almost blank about his message. Something that lacked his usual friendliness and humour.

You didn't tell her about us and our conversations, did you? I asked.

What conversations? he replied.

I was petrified, because my friend and great confidant was now playing games. This 'what conversations' sounded like a denial.

You said that we didn't have to tell our partners about our friendship, I replied, scorned.

I realized that his wife must have caught him red-handed. I decided that it was better to leave the situation alone.

A few days later, I went to the gym. A good sweat always allows me to let off some steam. I noticed his wife was there. The General's wife. Before, I barely knew of her existence, now she was like my shadow. I tried not to pay her any attention, and headed to the presses to give myself a good adrenaline boost, to get rid of my stress. As soon as I finished my first exercise, I saw the girl at the reception waving at me. I had no idea what the problem was, as I always left the apparatus clean and in working order. Yet the urgency was visible for the girl to talk to me. More curious than worried, I approached the counter.

"I'm sorry, ma'am, but we received a report by another attendee of the gym, with regards to your inadequate clothing. I have to ask you to leave the premises."

I looked at her in amazement. Okay my dress code did seem to be a bit provocative (I was wearing a tight crop top and shorts) but nothing that couldn't already be seen when walking around the center. In fact lots of people who came to the same gym dressed far more provocatively than I did. Some of their outfits were so tight I could see what they had for breakfast!

"Excuse me, but what about that girl? She's practically naked," I said, irritated, pointing to a hottie, who didn't have any problem showing off her thighs and abs in her skintight micro shorts and a top that left little to the imagination.

"Unfortunately we received a specific complaint about you, and we must act accordingly," the girl replied, red with embarrassment. She knew very well that she was talking shit.

"That's messed up. I have no intention of leaving. I've as much right to be here as anyone," I answered. Since it was a military gym, free for soldiers' wives, they called the military police and carabinieri to escort me to the door. I'll never know exactly if it was Henry's wife who created that unpleasant situation, but I wouldn't have put it past her.

To avoid further embarrassment, I decided that I had to talk to Adam, before he heard some rubbish from some old hag with a big mouth.

I hadn't even gotten home when my cell phone rang. It was Adam. He wanted to know what had happened at the gym. Some of his friends had witnessed the scene, and not having understood the dynamics, warned him. I simply told him we would talk about it immediately when he came home. I assured him I'd done nothing wrong, but still, I felt agitated. I didn't know what my husband was thinking. He must have thought it was something else, because as far as he was concerned, the 'thing' had ended, the moment he asked me to. I was afraid of getting into deep trouble. After all, we were talking about a general, who was the direct superior of my spouse.

Adam was furious with me. Not because of those small 'capers', but because he believed that I thought I was such a decorated woman.

"Did you think about going to bed with him? Like he really could have helped me in my career? It's crazy!"

"Of course not! Don't you realize that we are no longer targeted by lies and gossip?"

"Yes, but at what price? Replace one fat lot of gossip with more gossip, right?"

"No price. Henry was just a friend," I said.

"Henry?"

"That's his name."

Adam was irritated. He took on the tone of someone who has to explain something complex to a child. 'Em, okay! Lemme explain. The simple version. There's these little things called *military regulations*. Maybe you don't understand these, um, regulations, but dear Henry (he pronounced his name in a funny voice) does. I can't believe it! What have I ever done to deserve this, Eva?"

"Look, Adam, let's not overdo it now. Next time, instead of watching TV and not defending me in front of your family, remember that you should be the man I married, not only a good dad... Lately you're forgetting this..."

"Ah, obviously it's all my fault now? Wow, take that Adam! I get it, jeez..."

"It isn't your fault but you can't be mad at me for everything, every time! I felt lonely. I needed you and your support."

I also admitted that I had thought about using this friendship to make him jealous; praying every night for him to take my phone and spy on my conversations, then in a fit of jealousy, make love to me all night long. I wanted to feel as loved, as fresh as the day he sky-dived into my welcoming arms.

CHAPTER 38

TWO DAYS PASSED, IN total silence. My husband didn't want to talk to me. My illustrious, *supposed* friend was also ghosting me. I decided to write to Henry about how disappointed I was by his behavior, especially the suspicion I had about him, confessing everything to his wife. What made me laugh was how he responded; shooting a mountain of bullshit, turning the blame on me and making me out to be a stalker who had been persecuting him, when it was *him* who had been happily writing to me for six months; *him* who had friend requested me on Fakebook and *him* who had made lewd, intimate, unprofessional remarks. He'd been the one who approached me at the gym, like a predator with an angel face. I was offended. Once again my pride and honor had been betrayed by this so-called decorated person I had put all my trust in. Plainly, he was trying to take me for a fool!

Every day, it seems, we are forced to contend with powerful people and corporations who want to destroy us, who want to drive us insane, make our lives hell and want nothing less than to find a smoking gun next to our suicide note, spattered with our blood and brains. Every day, a new pointless, tiring war, a new threat, a new demon lying in wait, a new unhappiness. We only want the best for people, we only want to mutually respect each other; we only need to be appreciated and protected.

You know what?

The mere thought of having to go and see the Christmas Play at my daughter's school, having to sit right there next to this pair of deluded fools (Henry and Ms Sour Face) was something I couldn't stomach. As if that were not enough, a few days later, from out of nowhere, a new type of *Confessions* page on Facebook popped up, with the premise of making people talk *freely*. FFS! Thanks to anonymity it soon became another malignant den of cyber bullies and common charlatans; full of insane witches and weirdoes, snakes and serpants of all kinds; who spent their day to day lives, faking their Christian virtues, while in the evening, wallowing in their devilish deeds. In other words, it was a diabolical page of *filth*, fit for demons and no-one else!

So much illiterate crap was written there that it *defied belief.* Alongst all this colonic vilness was an anonymous post, dedicated to my misadventure at the gym, a rambling, piss poor, toxic, mispelled, ungramatical puzzle of batshit. It wasn't difficult to understand who could have written it, since he presented himself proudly as the promoter of my expulsion.

I decided to talk about the coming shitstorm with Roxanne. In the midst of that grotesque situation, she was my unique shelter, because she knew what it was like in that nest of vipers she worked for. She immediately gave me a huge rebuke, since she had always advised me against having relationships with people of dubious morality (she actually used very different terms). After she was done venting, the professional side of her took over again.

"Think about your husband. He's cornered now. What can he do? He sees his boss hitting on you, and cannot lift a finger. If Henry's tried it with you, he's done it before, and if he's done it before, he'll do it again! Here's the email of a senator who takes care of these abuses of power in the army. I've already talked to him for other reasons. He seems a reliable person to me. Explain it to him."

I felt a little nervous. A senator? In America it was normal procedure. I wasn't going to let a certain kind of 'shyness' prevent me from doing what was right and true. I had no time to lose. I swiftly wrote the letter. That letter somehow arrived at the Pentagon. It wasn't long before I received an answer. Not only was the senator very interested in my story, given the importance of the character involved, but he was also willing to talk to me personally. I should have done an interview first with some important American newspaper. We had to make a splash soon, or the army would swiftly sweep everything under the rug.

"I'm afraid they may try and cover it up inside the army base, where they scratch each other's back," the senator explained. "Anyway, I don't want reprisals against your husband. They can sure make life difficult and will do all they can, unofficially, to break you. To circumnavigate all these rocks, the best thing to do is to blow up the scandal from the outside."

In that sultry summer, I received a call from an American journalist of a well-known outlet, having received the word from the senator. The journalist explained to me how important it was, even in America, to blow the whistle on an affair like this, and that this kind of behavior now was so widespread, that they could no longer speak of a few bad apples. She pushed me to tell the whole story. Although I was wary at the beginning, I decided that since I had already taken one great step in coming forward, there was nothing else to fear.

The story also helped me. In those days, the Weinstein case was breaking, in which a Pandora's box of Hollywood's infamous casting couch secrets, which had once been common practice, was still very much in evidence all over the world; in all sectors and professions. Especially in Italy.

CHAPTER 39

THEY CALLED ME FROM the Pentagon one afternoon, requesting me to give my version of events, regarding the case of the General. They asked me if I would swear an oath to God.

"No problem!"

Over the phone they instructed me to repeat the verses. I swore to tell the truth and 'nothing but the truth, so help me God.' I don't fear God because I would have had to swear to God that my words were my beliefs. Apparently these Pentagon officials were in some office on the speakerphone. They introduced themselves: Colonel Phillie, a female captain (Kelly) and two others; the scribes. The first questions were very simple to answer because they were straight and detailed. Colonel Phillie asked, "Have you ever asked the General for money?"

"In what sense?"

I already knew that they were trying to save what little dignity was left of their beloved general.

"In the sense of money!" the Colonel reply. "Have you ever asked the General for money or gifts?"

They were trying to make me contradict myself, twist words that I didn't mean. They were really fantastic! They were pretty sure, they could manipulate me at their whim, with those questions. Perhaps they had underestimated me? They even asked me if I'd been coached by their government employee, Mrs. Roxanne Bass, and what my *relationship* was with her! In practice, this interview was turning against me and Roxanne. It was in that moment that I understood this was not going to go smoothly for me our Roxanne, I just pray that my husband's career could be sacrificed. I wondered did they understand that the General picked me despite my husband's career and my friendships on the base. I saw that "they" were attempting to change the direction, I later learned that the attacks would continue. I was getting tired of this game. I gave them the *coup de grace* when I answered their question about money. On my side of the line, I lit a cigarette.

"Money? So you want to know about money? I'll tell you about money. Do you have a sheet and a pen? I'll give you the password to my Facebook. I'll give you forty-eight hours. Then you can understand who I write to, what I write and what kind of woman I am. Most of all, I'll give you permission to read the *two thousand messages* that me and Henry have exchanged! Then you can see for yourself, that I never asked him for money or blackmailed anyone!"

There was silence for ten seconds. It was clear from the cough of embarrassment, that I had them cornered. They did not expect that I would walk in the light and the truth would not allow them to hurt me directly but they continued to try to put my light out. They attacked Roxanne too and released my name all over my little community, the covert procedures they used to damage me would later be revealed.

The General was removed and, I later learned, fired from the army. I hadn't blackmailed him. I hadn't gone looking for trouble. I hadn't wished for any of this to happen. At the same time, his accusations against me simply melted like snow under the sun. I had no remorse. I will not be tamed by the system. The General had played all his fake cards, swearing his loyalty to the principles of the American Constitution, but in his behavior with me, he *violated* the concepts of truth and responsibilities that are supposedly so sacred in America...

...it's here in America that my story must pause. I say *pause*, because it's not the end of the story, but the end of the book. What happens next in my story is up to developments much bigger and wonderous than I can imagine. I'm in America, not only to meet my destiny, but to share this story, share my love and to share my life with the family I have been blessed with and my treasured friends who have always stood by me. Always going forward. My memory, as it often occurs to me, sometimes becomes an invisible mist, that cowardly deforms the past. I have lived too many lives and too many experiences for my age. I have understood nothing of my life. Or everything. Every new day has yet to be constructed.

As for these returning ghosts, demons and angels; I have learned, with my sharp eyes, how to spot them, use them, be used by them and to learn their lessons. I don't feel like trying to understand the unknown. I want to advance it. I've often felt that there was a benevolent spirit walking with me, even when times were tough. The signs are there and we can feel them, as long as we aren't afraid. Remember this. When there is darkness, we can find the light. We only need to remember *who* the light is, for they will lead us out of the darkness.

If I have a talent for anything, it's the talent to recognise that I have always been true to myself and will battle for a better world, where women never have to be afraid again. I am Eva. You are Eva. My story does not end here and will not until the light shines so bright on them that no shadows are available to rely on.

About The Author

Michela Morellato was born in the beautiful Palladian city of Vicenza, Italy, where she was raised by her family of entrepreneurs. Her teenage years and studies were marked by a struggle to adapt to an unfortunate change in domestic prosperity, a refusal to conform to hypocritical traditions and a fierce desire to gain independence and control over her own destiny.

With a relentless, single-minded curiosity, Michela explored various career paths in the world of glamour and show business, more notably as a media commentator; turning in many appearances on national television in her native Italy. Her arresting looks, sharp wit and provocative 'giving it to you straight' opinions, made her as many enemies amongst the audience, as it did fans and admirers.

It was in this carnival society, where she mixed with the beautiful and the grotesque, the famous and the dangerous, the delicious and the disgusting; that she personally encountered and eventually exposed the not uncommon practises of sexual harassment. Indeed Michela, revealed this unpleasant convention to an indifferent Italian media, years before the fashionable #metoo and #timesup movements; long before the Weinstein allegations snaked over and through the Hollywood hills.

While 'Michela Morellato' may by synonymous in Italy with 'scandal', she has always sought to raise awareness about female empowerment, and call it out when she sees it; even in the most unlikely of places. Her recent proposal to 'Save Juliet' invited the public and politicians to reflect on the hidden meanings of the tourists' 'traditional' interaction with the Juliet statue in Verona.

Michela Morellato remains a controversial but stimulating figure within the Italian media and society. To many more, she is an enigmatic paradox.

She currently lives in Colorado with her husband, Adam, and her children Sveva and Ethan.